MELTING EVIE'S HEART

Film-set director Evie is between projects, and hurting from being dumped by the arrogant Marcus. Escaping to spend Christmas in her parents' idyllic countryside home, what will finally lift her mood — her mum's relentless festive spirit, the cosiness of village traditions . . . or the attention of gorgeous antiques dealer Jake? When the leading duo in this year's village pantomime drops out after a bust-up, Evie and Jake are roped in to take over. But with Evie playing the princess, just how seriously will Jake take his new role as Prince Charming?

JILL BARRY

MELTING EVIE'S HEART

Complete and Unabridged

LINFORD
Leicester

First published in Great Britain in 2019

First Linford Edition
published 2020

A catalogue record for this book is available
from the British Library.

ISBN 978–1–4448–4456–6

Published by
Ulverscroft Limited
Anstey, Leicestershire

Set by Words & Graphics Ltd.
Anstey, Leicestershire
Printed and bound in Great Britain by
T. J. International Ltd., Padstow, Cornwall

This book is printed on acid-free paper

1

I'm not too sure I should run away like this.

Evie Meredith sighed as she turned off the main road. She was coming to the Cotswolds to escape her London life, although it was still only early December. Usually she never got home for Christmas until the twenty-fourth, her birthday. Things were different this year.

Because she'd taken the short cut, her sat nav was advising her to make a U-turn.

'Get lost,' she told it. She needed to keep calm — or risk dissolving into a mass of jelly the moment she set foot inside her parents' house.

Evie slowed down and pulled off the road. Blinking back tears, she swallowed hard.

It's all over. He doesn't want you any

more. Which part of that do you not understand?

She was minutes from home. Rummaging in the door compartment, her fingers found a crumpled pack of paper hankies. A sob shook her. Why not have a good cry and be done with it?

The outburst didn't last long. She was mopping her eyes, blowing her nose and wondering whether her mascara had turned her into a Morticia Addams lookalike when a tap on the window startled her.

Horrified, she looked up to find a man peering in. Where the heck did he spring from?

She glared at him, vaguely registering how attractive he was. He straightened up at once, though he didn't back off. Evie clicked the door lock before winding down her window.

'Can I help you?' Her tone matched the icy outside air and she reached for her mobile phone. This stranger had better not have any weird ideas.

'I, um, stopped a few yards up the

road to answer a phone call. Then I noticed you pull in and wondered if you were all right. I apologise for startling you. Generally it's only we locals who use this road to Lower Mossford.'

'Which is possibly why I'm using it too? My parents live in the village.'

The stranger ran a hand through his slightly unruly thatch of dark hair. To her annoyance, she noticed his lips twitch.

'That would explain it then. But you — well, forgive me, but you seemed to be distressed.'

'It's my air freshener.'

'I'm sorry?'

'I have a new air freshener in my car. Arctic Pine — it's quite, um, pungent. It must've given me an allergic reaction.'

Her voice tailed off. He really had the most amazing eyelashes. You could almost shelter beneath them in a rainstorm.

'OK, well, I must get going. I'm glad you're all right.' He hesitated. 'I have

3

plenty of tissues in my car if you need them.'

'I'm almost home now.' She relented. 'Thanks for the offer. I'm sorry if I sounded offhand.'

'You've every right to be cautious with strangers. And I'm almost home too. Have your parents lived in the village long?'

She could swear he was trying to look down at her left hand. Was he checking if she wore a ring? Surely he wasn't about to ask her for a date? She didn't need this, unbelievable eyelashes or not.

'They moved in last spring. This will be their first Christmas in their new home.'

'Great! Well, take care. I suppose it's a little early to wish you the compliments of the season?'

Evie watched him walk back to his shiny black estate car. How had she not noticed it? Maybe because she'd been peering through a veil of tears. The man with the eyelashes and the dark chocolate voice waved as he glided past, and her eyes widened as she saw exactly what was stowed in the rear of his vehicle.

★　★　★

This route saved her driving through Upper Mossford, past the church, the village green and The Wheatsheaf — once the pub where farm workers, farriers and plumbers drank together. Now it called itself an old inn, drawing customers from miles around for its adventurous chef and scrumptious food.

She parked on her parents' driveway. One of her folks must be out — her mum, probably. She stretched before hurrying round to the back door. In the utility room she received a joyous welcome from Rusty, the family's red setter.

'Here's my baby! Have you missed me, then? I'm sure you've put on weight since I saw you last, you little terror!'

She straightened up as her father came in.

'Good journey?' Charlie Meredith, arms wide, beamed at his daughter.

She hugged him back. 'Not bad at all, thanks. A bit of a hold-up around Elmchester.'

Evie pulled a doggie chew from the pocket of her long silver-grey cardigan and offered it to Rusty. He padded straight back to his basket, bearing the treat. She laughed.

'He never quite believes I won't take it back.'

'I remember you being like that as a small girl, opening your gifts from Santa. You'd always hide them in your room when it came to bedtime. Your brother used to tease you.' He smiled.

They went into the kitchen. 'Yeah, I can vaguely remember hiding stuff. I think it was because the presents used to appear as if by magic.'

'Which was true, of course.'

'Absolutely. And I must have worked out that they might disappear again the next night. I wouldn't have put it past Ed!'

'Is it tea you're making?' Her father sank into the old rocking chair by the range.

'You bet. I stopped for a coffee and sandwich but a pot of tea sounds good.'

'Your mother left a lemon drizzle cake in the blue tin.'

'I'm surprised she found the time, with all she has on. When we last spoke, she said she'd taken over as chairman of the village hall committee.'

'Tell me about it! That, plus school governor, and her shifts in the community shop . . . '

'And you have gardening club and cricket club.'

'Not much doing this time of year, but I'm researching local history at last. I don't do much consultancy now, as you know. And you?' Her father cleared his throat.

'It's all right, Dad.' Evie set the kettle on the hotplate. 'Yes, I was gutted when

Marcus told me he needed to move on — '

'Stupid expression. Moving on, I mean.'

'I was upset, but no way would I have begged him to stay.'

'Jolly good thing too. Nothing but a bounder.'

Evie couldn't help smiling. It was easy to tell her father was a great fan of P G Wodehouse.

'So what about work, Evie? Will you still find yourself bumping into that despicable fellow?'

'My contract for the film has ended so hopefully not for a long while, by which time he'll have forgotten what I look like.' Evie opened the cake tin. 'Oh, yum.' She reached for plates, wishing her father would leave her alone to cope with the smarting wound of her broken relationship.

'Anything else in the offing? Another contract, I mean,' he added hastily.

'Possibly. I'm not planning to rush off soon, though. I hardly ever see you two, and I have loads of reading and box sets to catch up with, provided you and Mum can put up with me until after Christmas.'

'We might just manage.' He beamed. 'And there are one or two people around here who'll be delighted to see you. They always ask after you at The Wheatsheaf, as do the vicar and his wife.'

'I've been tipped off about a job working on a shoot in Switzerland in the New Year. It's a TV series about chalet maids, set in the Seventies. It sounds fun so I think I'll send in my CV.'

'But if you got it, would you keep your flat on? You still share with your old uni mate, I presume?'

'Of course. Ben and I get on fine and he jumped at the chance of moving his girlfriend in for the next few weeks. If I did happen to get the Swiss job, and she stayed on, I'd be covering my rent and when I got back . . . well, it's only what-ifs at the moment.'

'I've been looking forward to having you around. With your mother being here, there and everywhere, you and I might even get a game of Scrabble!'

The tea was brewing. The home-made cake smelled scrumptious and her mother had slathered it with glace icing in her usual enthusiastic way. Both her parents, wherever home might be, were always on her side. But after her hectic London lifestyle, would she feel restless after the first few days of rural peace and quiet?

★ ★ ★

'I'm happy to help with chores, Mum. You're probably up to your eyebrows with stuff so you may as well make use of me while you can.'

Evie and her parents were sitting around the dining table later that evening.

'Oh, I have other things in mind for you, Evie,' Helen Meredith said.

Evie didn't like that look on her

mother's face. She'd seen it many times. An image of the Bond villain stroking a white cat fluttered into her mind.

'Come on, Helen. The girl's hardly unpacked.'

Evie's mum ignored her husband. 'Having you here with time on your hands will be very useful, darling. The village hall committee want to encourage everyone to make this year a special one, with as many people as possible putting up their festive lights and decorations.'

'Your mother means both Upper and Lower Mossford. Apparently, we're duffers down here. The residents along the top road of the village are much more proactive.'

Evie sipped her wine. 'I'm not sure how I can help. I'm not even a resident.'

'Ah, but this is your home too, Evie,' her mother said. 'With your artistic flair, you should have plenty of brilliant ideas. Your father will give you a hand, of course.'

Evie and her dad exchanged glances.

'I think this could be a long night,' he said.

'I've decided to call a meeting on Tuesday evening,' Helen said. 'Chat over some ideas, arrange to help less mobile folk who might need help putting up festive wreaths or outside lights.'

'Isn't it rather short notice?'

'They can come here. I've made a list of likely folk.'

'Victims, you mean?' Charlie laughed.

His wife's hard stare would have turned a lesser man to stone. 'I was about to say, I'll put a notice in the shop and something on the website.'

'Mossford has its own website?'

'Of course. You should take a look, Evie. If we make a combined effort, the village will become a winter wonderland.'

'People never seem to have any time nowadays. Plus there's the expense involved, don't forget.' Charlie leaned back in his chair.

'It doesn't take long to fix a tree near a window so people can enjoy colour and sparkle in the winter gloom,' Helen said. 'I bet there are plenty of tree lights tucked away in attics. What we need is to get them out and working.'

'So what do you have in mind for me, Mum?'

She noticed her parents exchange glances. Meaningful ones. Her father was probably hoping to sit on the fence. Until his wife nudged him.

'You're friendly and capable of charming people to do your mother's bidding! Isn't that right, Helen?'

'Well, I wouldn't have put it quite that way, but it would be wonderful if you could knock on doors, Evie. Drum up some support. Ask if anyone needs help, that kind of thing.'

'So, is it just me you intend throwing to the lions or will I have company?'

'A man called Tom Vallance has volunteered to help. He runs an antiques business in Elmchester but he often works from home.'

Charlie Meredith leaned forward. 'Your mother and Tom often cross swords, just so you know.'

'As I was saying, he's agreed to knock on doors and push notes into letterboxes. So if we get him doing Upper Mossford, you could easily cope with our bit, Evie.'

'I'll do my best. Anything else?'

'The church Nativity tableau desperately needs some tender, loving care,' her father said. 'The figures are about three feet high and I can administer first aid but I'm no good at painting faces or sewing costumes.'

'Hey, they're not my speciality either. I just search out artefacts and decorate the set, remember? Occasionally I've known to bake a cake for an afternoon tea scene.'

'I remember spotting your Victoria sponge in that costume drama they filmed in Berkshire. Such a fabulous setting — everyone raved about that show. You're far more artistic than your father or me. Could you at least take a look?'

'It's ages since I went to church,' Evie said. 'The vicar's a nice man, though.'

'His wife's already sewing costumes for the annual pantomime. I know she'd be so relieved if you took the Nativity scene off her hands.'

Evie knew she couldn't escape.

'No pressure? OK, you win. I'll have a go.'

Maybe, with all this going on, I won't have time to mope when all my friends are buying frocks for Christmas parties . . .

★　★　★

She woke next morning, unsure where she was. Since her parents moved house, she'd only visited twice. The furniture and many other items were the same but there were new carpets, curtains and lampshades and her new bedroom felt oddly like a hotel room.

15

Still, the en suite bathroom was a bonus, and it would be fun to explore the village, even if with an unusual motive. She needed to know where to find that antiques dealer, too.

In the kitchen, she found her father grilling bacon. Since when did he start listening to Radio Two's Breakfast Show?

'Love the music, Dad. And that smells wonderful. Isn't Mum up yet?'

'Fuelled by two cups of Indian tea, she's printing out propaganda for you to hand out.'

Evie giggled. 'She certainly doesn't hang about, does she?'

'Has she ever? I still wonder how she managed to give birth to Ed and you precisely on the due date. You narrowly missed being born the day after your twin brother — but I might have known your mum would triumph.'

'I never knew that. How amazing!'

'Your mother's an amazing woman and she was probably Boudicca in a past life. Heaven knows what she ever

16

saw in me!' He gave the bacon slices a poke.

'I think you two are perfectly suited. You keep her anchored, and she . . . she . . . '

'She stops me from rusticating?'

'Maybe.' Evie filled the kettle. 'This village seems to have plenty happening. It's good that you're pleased with your new lives.'

'It takes a while to settle but we like our new abode and the locals are friendly.'

'They seemed to be last summer, when we went to The Wheatsheaf.'

'Meant to say, the landlord sometimes puts on a quiz night. The next one's tomorrow at half past seven if you fancy it. Your mother and I don't expect you to hang around here all the time, especially as we've already roped you in for some good deeds!'

'No offence Dad, but will I be the youngest there?'

'There's a pretty wide mix, according to our friendly landlord. Why don't I

17

walk you down tomorrow evening for a pint?'

'You're on, except I'm not a beer drinker. I used to go to quiz nights at my local in Fulham until . . . well, you know how things can change.'

'I do. And you know that old saying?'

'I don't know unless you tell me, Dad.'

Evie posted four slices of seeded bread into the electric toaster.

'They say there's only one cure for a man and that, my sweet, is another one!'

'Whoa, no way! I'm definitely not looking for another man. The last one was way too much trouble. I knew he had faults. We all have faults. But to dump me with absolutely no warning — it'll take Hell to freeze over before I'm stupid enough to trust a guy again. Especially one that's good-looking, so there!'

The toaster pinged as though applauding.

'I'm sorry, darling.' Evie's dad

18

switched off the grill. 'That wasn't the most tactful of remarks.'

'Don't worry. But just so you know, I'm definitely not in the market for a new boyfriend.'

Evie focussed her attention on making tea. She'd just remembered the man she encountered yesterday when she was in pieces. No way would she let an attractive guy turn her head again — even one who had incredible eyelashes.

2

The mild December weather encouraged Evie to set off on her mission. Armed with Helen's print-outs, she wriggled into her emerald green poncho, pulled a matching cap over her copper curls and put on her brown suede boots.

Smoke was drifting from the chimney of the first house she came to. This was wood-burner territory. The gardens were well tended and she hoped for positive reactions to the Christmas lights plan. But her thump to the brass doorknocker had no result. Evie knocked again and this time heard someone unlock the door before peering round it. The elderly resident regarded her with suspicion.

'Good morning, I'm sorry to interrupt your Sunday. I'm Evie Meredith from up the road.'

No reaction.

'My mother's on the village hall committee?'

Still no reaction.

Evie held out a flyer. 'I wonder if I could leave this. It's a request for help with this year's festive lights.'

The woman looked at the paper slip in Evie's hand and shook her head. 'I have my favourite charities and I don't give at the door, sorry.'

'Oh, no one's asking for money. I didn't mean that kind of help. Sorry, could I just give you this? We're hoping everyone will make a big effort and put their Christmas lights up this year. It's been a bit of a mixed one, don't you think? Nice to have something cheerful to think about . . . '

Stop gabbling!

The woman didn't even bother taking the flyer from Evie's hand. Instead, she frowned.

'I don't do Christmas. Thank you for calling.'

Evie faced a closed door. Not a good start.

She pushed flyers into the letterboxes of the next five cottages without knocking or ringing. There was a small development of more modern dwellings coming up and she decided to see if she could find anyone who might make her feel more welcome.

A young woman of about her age came to the door of the first house. She was cuddling a very young child in her arms and her face lit up at the sight of Evie.

'Hi, what can I do for you?'

Encouraged, Evie introduced herself and explained the plan.

'Fabulous,' said the young woman. 'I'm Kate, currently still on maternity leave, and with a husband working silly hours, so I'm definitely up for a project. Most of the young mums I know are back to work so I don't have much company.'

'You sound perfect for my mother's campaign. She's on the lookout for

22

younger villagers to help liven things up this Christmas. She knows she must tread carefully, in case anyone resents her chivvying them — new brooms and all that.'

'Wise lady! I remember when your parents were moving in. I was pushing the pram past and they both spoke to me. We hadn't long had Liam then.' She dropped a kiss on the baby's head.

'He's gorgeous,' Evie said. 'Look, Kate, may I leave you one of Mum's notes? If you can put a word in with your neighbours, that'd be much appreciated.'

Kate nodded. 'No problem. Next door are away this weekend but stick a note in their door and I'll tell them you've been round. I'll see if my mum will babysit on Tuesday so I can attend the meeting. Wills — that's my husband — has his hands full with the Mossford Manor Festive Fairyland.'

Wills and Kate? Really?

'Do you mean that house with the

wonderful old gateway on the other side of the village?'

'That's the one. The owners have taken on new staff and they're hoping to upgrade the house in the stately homes listings.'

'I must have a look round. I'm between jobs so I don't have to rush back to London.'

'Oooh, what I wouldn't give for a day's shopping there!'

Evie felt guilty.

'I s'pose I take that for granted. Sorry!'

'No worries. I wouldn't swap my two guys for all the designer boutiques in the West End. Look, Evie, if you fancy a walk up to the manor with Liam and me for coffee one morning, you know where to come. They should have the full festive works up and running by Wednesday, Wills said.'

'That sounds like even more reason to get the village into its party frock! Hopefully I'll see you on Tuesday evening then, Kate. Maybe fix a date for later in the week?'

Evie set off again, feeling more cheerful after meeting chatty Kate. If she could complete her visits to all the houses down here, she could call at Mr Vallance's house and hand over the flyers her mother intended for the upper level.

Before too long, she was walking past the village green towards a large house with a cedar tree dominating its front garden.

Evie walked through the open gates and crunched over the gravel towards the door. Its rather unusual shade of grey-green told her Mr Vallance hadn't nipped down to the nearest DIY store for any old can of gloss. She hadn't a clue how old the house might be, but its honey-coloured stone walls and mellow tiled roof would warm an estate agent's heart. Somehow, knowing he was an antiques dealer, she'd expected more lichen covering the brickwork and maybe a few gargoyles poking their tongues out.

She pressed the bell, trying not to giggle as the chimes rang out. She couldn't help picturing a stern-faced butler abandoning his silver polishing, and proceeding across the hallway, to discover who dared disturb the Sunday tranquillity. While waiting, she pulled the remaining bundle of paper slips from her bag, ready to hand over when the door opened.

She was unprepared to see a familiar figure.

'Well, hi.' The gorgeous man with the amazing eyelashes smiled at her. 'This is an unexpected pleasure.'

Don't blush. Just don't blush, you idiot!

Evie dropped her paperwork on the doorstep. Fortunately, her mother had secured the bundle with a sturdy rubber band.

'Whoops!' Evie was about to rescue the flyers, but wasn't quick enough. And those eyelashes looked even thicker and glossier, viewed from above their owner's dark head.

He stood up and examined the bundle in his hand before looking back at her.

'These are from my mother, Helen Meredith. She asked me to deliver them to Mr Vallance. Would that be you?'

'I'm sorry to disappoint you, but I do believe these might be intended for my father, Mr Tom Vallance.' His eyes twinkled mischievously and his warm gaze held hers while various parts of her anatomy woke up in a way she'd thought was consigned to history.

He was still staring at her. She cleared her throat. 'Well, if you could pass this lot on to your father, that would be most helpful.' She hoisted her shoulder bag and took a step back.

'I'm afraid he's a little under the weather at the moment. I'm never quite sure why we use that expression, are you? Pa's in a lot of discomfort with his back, but of course I'll make sure he gets what your mother's sent him.'

He was staring at her. Maybe that

was because she couldn't take her eyes off him.

Evie nodded. 'That's fine, but I'm so sorry to hear he's in pain. I suppose it's an occupational hazard?'

'Look, Miss . . . I mean Ms . . . Meredith — would you like to come in and talk me through whatever this is all about?'

'There's really no need, Mr Vallance. It's just a matter of distributing flyers to the houses in Upper Mossford and your father knows all about the project. But I can take those off you, if you like. I can just as easily deliver them later, now I've done with our part of the village.'

He was reading. 'Ah, so this is to do with Christmas lights and so on? Not pantomime business?'

'No. I mean yes, it's to do with lighting up Mossford.'

'I remember my father mentioning something. Look, I'll stuff these through people's letterboxes later. Unless . . . unless you'd like to keep me company?'

Tempting ... so very tempting, but ...

'That's kind but I must get back. Thanks again, Mr, erm, Vallance.' She began to walk away.

'Hey!' Evie stopped and turned round. 'I didn't mean to be presumptuous.'

Sad, puppy dog eyes. That won't work on me.

'And it's Jake, by the way.'

'My name's Evie.' *And if I don't get away quickly, I might implode with longing!*

'Good to see you again, Evie. Maybe our paths will cross on some future occasion?'

Capable only of nodding dumbly, she turned and sped off over the gravel. Why, oh why, couldn't she be left in peace to be miserable? Jake Vallance was obviously a high-flyer and even more attractive than her ex. But if he thought this fairy lights frenzy would draw her and him together, he was totally mistaken.

On Monday evening, Evie's dad escorted her to the pub where Gareth, the landlord, greeted her like a long-lost friend.

'Can you stay for the quiz?' Gareth glanced at the clock. 'We're off in a few minutes and we're one short in Team Six.'

Evie's dad shook his head. 'I'm hopeless at these things. Evie, why don't you step in?'

'I'll have a go, but who's on Team Six, Gareth? If it's three sharp players, they're probably better off without me.'

'Nah, these boys are left over from the cricket club meeting earlier. They could use your help.'

'Cricket? In December?'

'They're planning their Valentine's dinner dance. I gather it helps keep their wives and girlfriends happy, something to look forward to in dreary February.'

'OK. As long as they don't mind a

mere woman joining them. Are you staying, Dad?'

Evie picked up her lime and soda. Her father was enjoying his usual half pint of local ale.

'I don't think so. I'll finish this then get back. Why don't you text me when you're ready and I'll collect you.'

'OK, if you're sure.' Evie shifted slightly to one side, sensing someone standing behind her.

'Just the man,' the landlord boomed cheerfully. 'Jake, meet your new team member. This is Evie.'

She swung round to find herself face to face with Jake Vallance for the third time in forty-eight hours. What's more, he looked highly amused.

'We must stop meeting like this! So you're coming to help us out then, Evie?'

'Well, I . . . '

Jake held out his hand to her father. 'Mr Meredith, I believe. My father tells me you too are a fan of his favourite author?'

31

'Yes, we're both Wodehouse geeks.' Evie's dad looked pleased. 'I hear Tom's under the weather? My wife will miss sparring with him at the next committee meeting!'

'He does enjoy an argument and his back's been playing him up for a week or so, which makes him very grumpy, I'm afraid.' Jake looked over his shoulder. 'The natives are becoming restless. I'm supposed to be getting this round in. What would you like, Evie?'

She indicated her glass. 'I'm good, thanks.'

'Maybe having one team member sober will be an advantage. Same again, Gareth, please. Though why I come in here, only to be jeered at because Wales beat England last time they played, I'll never know.'

First cricket, now rugby. Fat chance she had of answering any quiz questions correctly.

Evie glanced at the two men at Jake's table. They were laughing and joshing together. What on earth had she let herself in for? But one part of her couldn't resist the chance to get to know Mr Jake Vallance a little better. Doing the job she did, it was always good to keep an eye open for contacts within the antiques trade. You never knew how useful they might prove.

As soon as she arrived at the table, Jake introduced his two mates as Lester and Wills.

'Do you happen to be the Wills who's married to Kate?'

He raised his eyes heavenwards. 'Do I look like one of the Royals?' He chuckled and offered his hand. 'My missus mentioned you. You made quite a hit, Evie.'

'She's lovely. So's your little boy. Hopefully we'll see something of one another.'

Lester grinned at her. 'All right?'

'I'm good, thanks.' Evie began to think the evening might not be a total washout after all.

The guys wanted to know what her specialist subject was and she made up all kinds of weird topics from dowsing to the nocturnal habits of dachshunds. This broke the ice and she heard Lester tell Wills he thought the new girl was all right for a townie.

The cheerful landlord rang a small brass bell. 'Five minutes, ladies and gentlemen. We're off in five minutes.'

Jake leaned towards Evie. 'I hope you don't mind me asking a personal question?'

Evie froze. He didn't waste much time!

'What's that fabulous perfume?'

She felt a tug somewhere that had no business feeling tugged. And she'd just been wondering what sexy aftershave he used.

'It's a blend,' she said quickly. 'Carnations, oranges, bergamot . . . a bit of this, that and the other. A friend in the trade concocted it.'

'I'm impressed. Does it have a name?'

'My friend christened it Evie.'

'Lucky girl, to have such a talented

friend.' He nodded towards the bar. 'I think we're at the starting gate now.'

Evie gathered her wits. Or tried to. Meanwhile, the landlord rang his bell again and they were off. All kinds of questions were thrown at the teams as everyone listened to the quizmaster.

'Mr Jaggers and Abel Magwitch,' Jake repeated after a literary question. 'I haven't a clue which book they appear in.'

Evie had volunteered to write down their team's answers. 'It's *Great Expectations*.'

'Yay! The girl knows her Dickens,' Lester said.

'Not all of them,' Evie said. '*Great Expectations* just happens to be one of my favourites.'

She groaned as the landlord read out the next question. 'In the film *The Bridge on the River Kwai*, who played the role of Commander Shears?'

'I bet Dad would know. He watches loads of old movies.'

'I know it too.' Jake grinned. 'My dad

likewise. It was William Holden.'

'Great.' Evie wrote down the star's name. The next few questions were, as she'd feared, about rugby, football and cricket. But her team-mates knew their stuff.

'And now for our last question, ladies and gentlemen,' warbled the Welsh landlord at last. 'How many times has Serena Williams won the Australian Open ladies' tennis championship?'

All three men groaned.

Evie punched the air. 'Seven times. Trust me.' She wrote down the answer.

Lester pushed back his chair. 'That deserves a celebration and it happens to be my round. What would you like to drink, my sweetheart?'

She noticed Wills's frown and sensed Jake, seated on her right, cringing. She decided to give as good as she got.

'That depends on what we're celebrating, Lester, my love! No one knows who's won yet.'

A snort from Jake. A slow smile of approval from Wills.

'A scratch team like us and we found answers for every question. Come on! You're one of us now, Evie.'

'Aw, thank you. I'd like a small glass of white wine, please.'

Her new friend whispered in her ear.

'Sorry, Evie. I was out of order. You're a star.'

Lester moved away and Wills excused himself, leaving Evie and Jake alone.

'You really did well, you know.'

'I got a little lucky. You guys answered questions I found totally baffling.'

He was gazing into her eyes. Again. Her tummy lurched. Jake Vallance had no right to be so drop dead gorgeous, or to have a voice that made her think of melting chocolate. She felt like a kitten, purring in sunshine. This on only her third night back home and before she even drank any wine.

'I don't care whether we win or lose,' Jake said. 'We certainly haven't disgraced ourselves.'

'Don't forget those tricky questions about former Prime Ministers.' Evie glanced at the window tables. 'One or two people were smirking over those. Obviously better at history than I am.'

She glanced at the bar. 'I'll stay and be sociable, now Lester insists I have a drink. But then I'll text my father so he can collect me.'

The moment the words left her mouth, she regretted them. How blatant did that sound! Sure enough, Jake wasted no time.

'I planned on walking home so I'm happy to escort you, Evie. It would save dragging your father out. Why not text him and say you're sorted?'

Sorted? She was far from sorted. Evie's glass of wine arrived. Grateful for the diversion, she joined in the jokey toasts Wills and Lester were proposing, and swallowed a mouthful of chilled white burgundy, still agonising over whether to accept Jake's offer.

If she insisted on texting her dad, Jake might think she didn't trust him — or decide she didn't possess a mind of her own. Neither of those options appealed.

But if she let Jake walk her home — it was out of his way, of course — and he asked her for a date, she feared she might not be able to refuse.

He was giving her that impish look of his again.

For goodness' sake, you're a grown woman, Evie. So, behave like one!

She was about to accept his kind offer. Her hand was fingering her mobile phone, lying beside her wine glass, when the door opened to admit a vision of loveliness.

She recognised the actress immediately. The woman was often cast in the role of a sexy temptress, or a 'flighty baggage', as her dad might say. But in the world of television, soap star Melissa McDonnell-Brown was known as Sweet 'n' Sour, with the accent on the sour. Evie had worked on the same show at the start of her career; she doubted Melissa would remember.

As Evie turned to speak to Jake, she realised his attention was totally focussed on the new arrival.

3

'Sweetie! I haven't seen you in ages. How are you?' Melissa called.

She had casually tousled honey-blonde tresses and clever cosmetics to give her complexion that no-make-up effect. A red fox fur tippet nestled around the actress's creamy neck, with a sugared almond-pink cashmere sweater hugging her voluptuous curves. Black leggings tucked inside high-heeled grey suede boots completed the outfit.

Wills' jaw was on the floor. Lester looked as though he'd been dive-bombed by a jet. As for Jake, the terrified look on his face puzzled as much as it delighted Evie. Because the jet was making a beeline for their table!

Have I misjudged her? Maybe she actually remembers meeting me at the television studios.

Evie, fascinated by the reactions of the men, braced herself. Only to be ignored.

'It is Jake Vallance, isn't it? I'm such a ditzy lady. Tell me I'm not mistaken, darling!'

Evie's heart stopped beating, recognised it was falling down on the job, and began following the script again. She sat back in her chair while Jake rose to receive a hug from the woman who made headline-hitting look easy.

Why wouldn't she? Most of us wouldn't want to be in that kind of situation!

Evie wondered why she felt so miffed. She was off men, wasn't she? So what bothered her? With any luck, she could slip out and text her father.

On second thoughts, what stopped her from walking home on her own? This was Mossford, not some dodgy corner of London. But Jake was asking if she'd like another drink and Melissa's smile was curdling.

'No, thanks, I need to get home. You

stay and catch up with Melissa. Thanks for a fun evening.'

'I'd love a glass of red, Jake darling.' The actress looked Evie in the eye for the first time.

Still hoping Melissa wouldn't remember her, Evie almost giggled as she realised Jake's eyebrows were sending her distress signals. She muttered a farewell to the actress and slipped past him as he approached the bar. She'd got through the door and messaged her father, saying she didn't need a lift, when she heard someone call her name. Evie whirled round.

'Hey, d'you want some company? I'm walking your way.'

Wills stood there. She'd never been so pleased to see anyone in her life before.

'That'd be great. It was a nice evening, but . . . '

'I know it's still early, but when I come to the pub, I like to get back and spend an hour with Kate before bedtime. And you looked as though you'd had enough.'

They began walking away from the old stone building, coloured fairy lights twinkling from inside its windows. At least the landlord and his wife didn't need coaxing into the Christmas spirit. Evie looked up and saw a dark velvet sky sparkling with stars. Will followed her gaze.

'I bet you don't get skies like that in London.'

'No, indeed.'

'Kate would kill me for asking, but are you and Jake an item?'

'Whatever makes you think that? I don't mind you asking but the answer's a definite no. We only met the other day.'

'It's just — when Melissa what's-her-name came on to him, I wondered if you were upset and decided to get out of the line of fire.'

Evie turned her head as she heard an owl hooting. On the hunt for prey.

Will seemed to read her thoughts.

'That owl will have its talons into

some creature before long. Reminds me of her back there!'

Evie chuckled. 'I'll pretend I didn't hear that. I met her once, you know. In London when I was working on the same show as she was in.'

'Are you an actress, then? Blimey, not two luvvies living in the same village?'

'No way! I'm a set decorator. One of the guys that find all the items needed to make a scene authentic. So, framed family photos, tea caddies, teddy bears, laptops, cereal bowls — everything we all have in our own homes, and plenty of unusual items as and when necessary.'

'I've never thought about all that sort of stuff.'

'It's interesting work. You meet all kinds of people.'

'I can imagine. So, how did you come to meet Jake? Kate says you haven't been around much since your parents moved in.'

Evie knew that all newcomers' lives were of huge interest to the locals, It probably took years before the villagers peeled off that incomer label. She didn't mind. But no way would she confess to parking in a gateway and bursting into tears because a love rat had given her the heave-ho.

'After I delivered those flyers round Lower Mossford, I took a bundle up to Mr Vallance's house and Jake answered the door. His father's laid up with a bad back and Jake volunteered to deliver the rest. My dad kind of volunteered me to join your team this evening, so now you know.'

'Ah, so when Madame La Guillotine came through the door, and happened on Jake, you decided to slope off, but you weren't upset?'

Evie smiled to herself. She could see why Kate and Wills were happy together.

'That's right. I wasn't sure if she'd remember me, but it was a relief to find she hadn't.'

'I'm not sure Jake, poor guy, would agree with you! Any man looking at that

Melissa would know she's trouble.'

'Maybe he was flattered she recognised him?'

Wills roared with laughter. 'No way! After she and her then boyfriend moved into the village, they threw a party in the pub. Jake didn't want to know. He told me he'd heard enough of her lifestyle to put him off for good.'

'But she must have met him before. How else would she know his name?'

'The antiques business. She and her man were trawling for stuff to furnish their new love nest. You remember the guy who played a baddie in that Sunday night bonnets and capes thing? Kate made me watch it,' he added hastily.

Evie thought. 'I know who you mean. I didn't realise she'd split from him.'

Why would I? Marcus was the only man on my mind for ages.

'Well, he and Melissa bought some items from Jake's father's shop in Elmchester. My wife read about them in one of those celebrity magazines.

Jake must have been in the shop at the time.'

Evie and Wills were descending the slope to Lower Mossford. It had quite a gradient, and made Evie wonder how everyone coped if heavy snow hit the village. She felt she ought to defend Melissa, because everyone knew you shouldn't believe everything you read in the papers, but didn't really feel like it. After all, if the star was looking for another boyfriend and Jake was interested, there didn't appear to be any rivals.

'My lovely wife tells me you and she might come up to the manor soon. Kate always likes to check out the decorations and this year of course, it's our little lad's first Christmas.' There was no mistaking the pride in Wills' voice.

'He's a gorgeous baby. You two are very lucky.'

Whoops, where did that come from? Evie had steeled herself not to think about weddings and nest building.

Marcus had made it plain he wasn't a settling-down kind of guy. She just hadn't anticipated how abruptly their relationship would end. She focussed on Wills talking about how Kate found being at home a little limiting.

'That wife of mine's a trained podiatrist, you know,' he said, again with pride.

'Wow, that's a great career. I'd have thought she could set up her own business when the time's right. Pick and choose her working hours?'

'That's the plan. Sadly Liam only has one granny living locally as my mother decided to go and live in Spain with her sister. They're both widows and they love the Mediterranean climate so can't say I blame Mum for moving.'

'Nice to have holidays with her, I expect?'

'You bet. After the baby was born she came to stay for a couple of weeks. We'll take him over there when he's older.'

They'd arrived at Rowan Cottage.

Wills reached over the gate and opened it for her.

'Thanks again for your company, Wills. By the way, did you find out which team won the quiz? I slipped out before Gareth announced it.'

'Two retired couples who've lived in the village for years. Nice folk. But us lot came second. I should've said. We lads decided it was right for you to have the prize. I think Jake said something about calling round and presenting it to you.'

⋆　⋆　⋆

Jake wasn't thrilled to find himself left holding the baby. Not only was he the only one of the runner-up team left to accept the second prize of a box of liqueur chocolates, he was sitting next to the wrong woman at the table.

Melissa had claimed the seat just vacated by Evie. Her perfume was as blatantly sexy as Evie's was delicate, evoking the heady scent of tropical blooms rather than wild flowers and summer rain.

'Oh, it's such bliss to be in the countryside again! Thanks for the drink, darling.' Melissa raised her glass to her incredibly plump pink lips.

'Your good health.' Jake took a swallow of lager. The woman was, after all, a customer of his dad's shop. Business was business. And Evie hadn't hung around. She obviously had something, or someone, more important than him to get back to.

He felt a wave of relief when Melissa sipped her wine and confided, 'I'm glad I popped in. My boyfriend's on his way here from Florida and he's driving down from Heathrow in the morning. He's in the market for some bits and pieces he'd want shipped back to New York. I've told him about the wonderful Vallance's Emporium so we'll be over to see you and your delightful dad soon.'

Jake nodded. 'We'll look forward to seeing you both. I'll make sure to have the coffee brewing.'

Her laughter tinkled. She patted his arm. 'Can't wait, darling. Now, tell me, that girl who was here when I arrived. I'm trying to think where I've seen her before. Can you tell me what her name is?'

Jake hesitated. Whatever Melissa's motive, he had no intention of becoming involved. What if Evie didn't want to be identified? He hadn't a clue what she did for a living and while he longed to get better acquainted, taking part in a pub quiz was hardly the best scenario for a quiet chat. What if something had happened involving the two women? He knew which one he'd rather protect.

'Um, d'you know, it's slipped my mind already. She only joined us at the last minute and my team mates were joshing with her, so I'm afraid I can't help you with that one.' He took another swallow of lager and looked at his watch. 'Ms McDonnell-Brown, I'm afraid I have to get back for a business call from a client in Montreal and he likes to use the landline.'

Melissa pouted. 'Such a pity.' Her gaze was already elsewhere. 'But that gorgeous cricket captain just caught my eye! I must say hello.'

Jake got to his feet. Melissa rose, glass in hand and planted a kiss on his cheek.

'I'll see you soon, darling. Ciao!'

He watched her flick her hair back, then undulate between the tables, flashing her radiant smile at the people seated at them. She knew how to work a room. And she was about to make the cricket captain's night, given he was a big fan.

Jake's lips twitched as he wondered whether the captain's wife would enjoy hearing how her husband had been singled out for attention from the red-top newspapers' favourite man eater.

He picked up the carrier bag containing the box of chocolates. This was the perfect excuse to call on the girl who'd so suddenly appeared in his life.

But should he mention Melissa's request for information, or should he forget it ever happened?

4

'Wow, Dad, these are lovely — but I see what you mean about them needing some tender, loving care.'

Evie was examining the wooden figures her father had unearthed from the back of the church. A lot of thought had gone into making them but the faded paint and torn garments gave them a sad, abandoned appearance.

'I brought the car because we'll have to take them home to work on. No way do I want to keep moving them around with choir practice and Sunday School going on.'

'You surely don't have room for all these in your shed?'

'No, but while I'm working on one, the others can stand in the utility room and wait their turn.'

'Hmm. Actually, I'm sure Mum won't mind as it's part of the whole

Christmas scene.'

'The most important part, in my opinion. Lights are all very well, but if we make a good job of these, folks will get a lot of pleasure out of them, especially when the church is candle-lit.'

'I hope there's a good turnout for Mum's meeting this evening. She'll be so disappointed otherwise.'

Her father grunted. 'Come on then, Evie. We'll take the figures out the back door. The vicar kindly unlocked it while you were gazing at the stained glass, he said he'd be back soon to lock it again so we'd best get a shift on.'

Very gently, Evie tried lifting the baby's mother.

'OK. I can manage this lady on my own.'

'If you're sure then, but maybe better leave the crib and baby to me. Be careful if you lift the sheep — you'll find more than one wobbly leg.'

'Come on then, Mary.' Evie hoisted her up in her arms.

Her father lifted Joseph. 'Let's stand

them by the door. I'll open the hatchback and load up.'

Evie followed him. 'I hope Mum's kept those blue curtains from my old bedroom. They'll be perfect for the Madonna's robe.'

'I'll be surprised if she hasn't.' He was already heading back to collect the crib.

Evie stood for a moment, gazing round. The peacefulness tempted her to linger and forget the outside world. But that wasn't going to happen.

Afterwards, she wondered if she'd had some sort of premonition. Because the front entrance door, unlocked while the. vicar flitted between vicarage and church, opened to admit a figure dressed in a white faux fur coat over long black patent leather boots.

'Hi there, folks! I thought it was time I took a peek at this fabulous old church.'

Evie tried to hide her dismay.

'Good morning, Ms McDonnell-Brown.'

Melissa looked equally disenchanted. 'Oh, so it's you again! Jake Vallance's little friend.'

Evie glared. She didn't need to be spoken to like this. She was no longer under contract and didn't intend letting the actress trample over her.

'I'm not his little friend, actually. May we help you with anything? The vicar will be back soon if you wish to speak to him.'

Melissa began walking up the aisle.

'Ooh, I feel positively bridal. If I decide to marry Bradley, we must definitely tie the knot here.'

She paused, hands on hips and stared at Evie, who'd seen her on set in that particular pose on several occasions. Evie waited, almost expecting to hear the actress yell, 'Get out of my church!'

'I know you from somewhere. Don't play tricks with me, darling. I'm not in the village much these days, but somehow I think we've met before . . . maybe it was in town. Am I right?'

'I've dressed several sets for scenes

58

you've been in. So, yes, it would've been in London. Fancy you remembering.'

'Ah, I've got it!' Melissa grinned. 'You're the poor girl Marcus dumped. Mind you, lots of people were surprised you lasted as long as you did. With a job like his, and those looks, he can take his pick. But I'm so sorry, darling. Next time, maybe find a boyfriend who's not out of your league.'

Evie seethed. But she wasn't about to slap anyone's face, however provoked.

'Thanks for the advice. Now I must get on. Some of us take village life seriously.'

Evie turned and walked back up the aisle.

★   ★   ★

'She's such a horrible person, I doubt she even bothered to read your flyer.' Evie stopped sewing a seam and glared at her mother.

'Still a shame you didn't remind her.'

Helen Meredith was stacking cups and saucers.

'Truly, Mum, you're better off without involving Melissa. How many dozens are you expecting, anyway? Aren't you being a bit optimistic?'

'We should have at least six, plus us. But the more the merrier. Our local celebrity does seem to have wound you up, though.'

'Let's just say our paths have crossed before and leave it at that.' Evie cut off a thread and held up the finished garment. 'What do you think?'

'I've always thought you inherited your gran's nimble fingers. That robe looks beautiful. How long until your father's mended the figure?'

'Mary's the least damaged so he may have her ready sooner than he initially thought. I noticed how he wolfed down his tea to head back out.'

'Do you want to show her off at the meeting?'

'I think it's probably best to keep the Nativity Tableau under wraps for the time being. I have a few surprises I want to try when the figures are back in the church and I'd prefer not to have people calling in to check on me.'

Helen raised her eyebrows as the hall phone rang. 'I hope this isn't someone giving apologies.' She hurried out.

Evie rose and carefully folded the cerulean blue robe. She couldn't seem to banish thoughts of Jake. It had been surprisingly awful at the pub, watching Melissa charm him. She'd even tried her wiles on Marcus once, when Evie was with him. At that time he'd been besotted with Evie, but couldn't resist playing up to the star for a while.

Evie had been devastated until Marcus assured her she was his one and only true love and hey, a bit of flirting never harmed anyone.

Foolish Evie! I was so naïve. She should have taken note of the signs then. Too late now.

Her mother came back in.

'That was Jake Vallance.'

'Right.' *I really couldn't care less.*

'Such a charming young man . . . his father's still having back problems so Jake rang to say he's standing in for him.'

'Jake is coming to the meeting? This evening?'

'Do you have a problem with that? Your father mentioned you two were on the same quiz team.'

'It doesn't bother me if Jake's here or not.' Evie tried to sound casual. 'As a matter of interest, why is he living with his folks? According to their firm's website, Jake's based in London and he does most of the travelling.'

'Ah, so you've checked him out, then?'

'Spare me that knowing face, Mum!' But Evie couldn't help laughing. 'As I told Dad, I've become disillusioned about men with movie-star looks, thanks very much.'

'If you say so, dear. You have to admit Jake's — what do you say nowadays? Fit? Buff?'

'Whatever! That's why I don't want

to know. Shall I fire up the coffee machine now? I can make a pot of tea once we know who wants what.'

'It's so good to have you home, Evie. It'll all work out in the end, you know. Trust me.' Helen hurried off, saying something about putting on her face, before her daughter could protest.

Evie sped upstairs when her mother returned, loosened her copper hair from its scrunchy and began brushing it so it hung in loose waves on her shoulders. She hesitated, then picked up her perfume spray and wafted a drift above her head, allowing the fragrance to settle. She was hardly back in the kitchen when the doorbell rang and she heard both her parents greeting the first arrivals, offering to take coats and chatting about the unpredictability of local weather forecasts.

Her phone buzzed. Evie picked it up to find a text from her new friend, letting her know she couldn't make it as she'd come down with a nasty head cold. Evie tapped out a quick *get better soon* message to Kate and walked into the hallway. Hearing the crunch of feet on gravel outside, she opened the door to find Jake Vallance.

'Hello again, Evie.'

'Oh, hello, erm, Jake. Do come in.' She held the door wider. He stepped inside and wiped his boots on the doormat.

'Shall I take your coat?'

He handed her a carrier bag.

'Your prize. Our team came second and the boys and I thought you should have it.'

She peered inside. 'That's a lovely thought. Thank you.'

He shrugged off his waxed jacket and unwound his stripy scarf. 'I hope I'm not late?'

Evie restrained herself from burying her nose in his scarf. *What's wrong with me? If only he didn't make my pulse race so . . .*

'You're not late. Let me hang up your coat, then we'll go through to the sitting room.'

She was acutely aware of him walking behind her. It was as though every inch of her skin tingled, longing for his touch. Her throat was dry and she needed to moisten her lips with her tongue.

The door to the big sitting room was ajar. Evie pushed it open and Jake signalled her to go ahead of him. She wanted to pull him back, grab his hand and rush him away to the conservatory to watch the starry sky with her and Rusty . . .

Who was she kidding? She wanted to feel Jake's arms hugging her close. Yearned to feel the warmth of his lips against hers.

'Ah, good to see you, Jake.' Charlie Meredith ambled over to shake the new arrival's hand. 'I hope that father of yours is doing as he's told.'

'Not according to my mother, Mr Meredith.'

'Please call me Charlie. And I think you've already met my wife?'

'Indeed I have. I gather you do a

great job of keeping my father in order on the village hall committee, Helen?'

The doorbell rang. 'I'll go,' Evie said.

When the village postmistress was settled beside Jake on the couch, Evie took orders for hot drinks and sped away. She was about to pick up the teapot and fill four mugs when there was a tap on the half-open door.

'Come in, Dad! I know it's you.'

Evie's father was known to play tricks, so she didn't look up until her visitor cleared his throat.

'I offered to bring this tray back.'

There was no mistaking that dark velvet voice.

'I'm so sorry! My father likes to play the prankster.' She busied herself with the tray.

'Evie . . . I wanted to get you on your own.'

'These teas can go in now. People can put their own sugar in.'

'I know we got off to a bad start. I intruded on your space last Saturday and I'm sorry.'

She moved over to the worktop. 'I'll pour coffee for you and me. That's everyone, then.' She guessed her cheeks probably matched the scarlet swirls on the silver coffee machine.

'When you brought those leaflets to the house I chickened out. And everything went pear-shaped after the quiz and you vanished like Cinderella's sequins at midnight.'

She turned towards him, holding two mugs of coffee. 'These will be getting cool.'

'Of course.' He frowned. 'You're trembling. Evie. Please tell me if I can help in any way.'

Evie said the first thing that came into her head.

'Thanks, but I'll leave you to it now. It's time I checked on my baby.'

★   ★   ★

In the conservatory, snuggled into the wicker couch with the dog curled up beside her, she realised she'd behaved very rudely. Jake would be in the sitting room by now and her coffee would be waiting in the kitchen. She just needed a moment to clarify her thoughts. She began stroking the dog's silky head.

'Tell you what, Rusty, my brain and my heart are definitely not speaking to each other. Why else would I suffer from these awful symptoms? Except they're not awful — sometimes what I feel is amazingly lovely. But I felt like this the first time I set eyes on Marcus and look where that got me. I couldn't bear to go through all that again.'

The red setter gazed at her mournfully.

'But if Jake walked through that door now, Rusty, I know what I'd want to happen. And that frightens the living daylights out of me.'

★   ★   ★

Jake took a mug of coffee and headed back to the meeting. His head was still swimming after Evie's startling

68

announcement. She had a baby? Was she married? He didn't recall seeing a ring on her finger and he'd taken a look last Saturday while she was sitting in her car, talking to him through her half-open window. He didn't care whether she was a single mum, but he did care if she was married — especially if there was a man in her life who didn't treat her properly.

Yet Evie obviously didn't want to be around Jake for longer than necessary.

His host was holding the sitting room door open. 'Where's Evie go to?' he asked.

'Um, she was going to check on her baby — '

But Charlie Meredith hadn't heard. He was passing a mug of tea for the postmistress and this was no time to speak of personal matters.

Helen was asking how people felt about the lights project. 'We need to crack on with it. It's lovely to see you all here and I want to thank you for sparing the time.' She looked around.

'We're ten in number altogether and if each one of us can coax a friend or neighbour to take part, that'll make a big difference for sure.'

'The village did look a bit dismal last year.'

Murmurs of agreement, then someone said, 'I think it's a great idea, making this a community thing. Why don't we all agree to switch on our lights at the same time?'

Clearly, everyone liked that suggestion. Voices he didn't recognise were still chipping in.

Jake was still lost in his own thoughts. He heard the vicar's wife saying she'd ask her husband to announce the date at the Sunday service and they could also publicise it on the community website. What was all that about?

He pulled himself together as he noticed Evie come in. She must have forgotten to collect her coffee. People were smiling at her. She lit up the room even if she didn't realise it. He ached to whisk her away somewhere he could take her in his arms so the two of them could talk.

'I need to give you Kate Warner's apologies,' Evie was telling everyone. 'She's come down with a cold but I know how keen she is to join in. She told me once her husband and his team have the manor house lights and displays up and running, he'll be able to help anyone having problems.'

'Such a nice young couple, William and Kate,' the postmistress said. She'd moved to sit next to the vicar's wife.

Others were commenting so Jake took the opportunity to hurry to the kitchen to fetch Evie's mug. 'Do you need sugar?' he asked.

Evie looked up, a startled expression on her face. 'I don't take it.'

'Same here.'

'Thank you for rescuing my coffee.'

She was still looking at him. His heart was thumping fast. Her eyes were the grey of storm clouds and her perfume drifted into his nostrils. For long moments he felt dizzy with desire.

'Baubles,' barked the postmistress. 'The bigger and shinier the better, and plenty of 'em. It's not just about lights.'

'We could certainly do with some more decorations for the tree that's being delivered to the church tomorrow,' said the vicar's wife. 'Any contributions welcome.'

He was hearing the conversation as though standing at the end of a tunnel. Jake swallowed hard and stood back. Could Evie sense it too? That indefinable feeling he hadn't experienced in years had hit him the moment she grudgingly wound down her car window.

He couldn't fight it. Didn't want to. She was walking over to the vacant couch and before he could change his mind, he was following her. Baby or no baby, he wanted her in his life.

5

Evie was the village shop's first customer next morning. She selected two lemons and a small jar of Cotswold clover honey to deliver to Kate, while fielding questions about her job and how long she was staying.

To her relief, another customer arrived and the conversation turned to the senior citizens' Christmas lunch.

How, she wondered, did Jake cope with people's interest in his personal life? Had he been born in Mossford? Last night, they barely exchanged a word while sitting together. But she'd felt a frisson of something when they locked gazes in the kitchen. She was pretty certain he felt it too.

When everyone got up to leave, the postmistress came over and began chatting so excitedly, Evie hadn't the heart to interrupt. Then her father had sought out Jake and the two of them appeared to be hatching something together. Just as their conversation ended, her mother brought Jake his coat and scarf and he'd glanced Evie's way, raised a hand in farewell and left.

It was probably for the best. He must surely have a girlfriend in London? Evie set off towards the lower village. The temperature had plummeted overnight, making her glad she was wearing the woolly hat she'd never think of wearing in London. She wondered if snow was forecast, but she didn't stop until she reached Kate's house.

Kate took a while to answer her ring but Evie could hear the baby crying and his mum calling to him. She eventually came to the door looking thoroughly sorry for herself and well wrapped up, with a pink mohair scarf snug around her neck.

'Sorry to take so long, Evie,' Kate croaked. 'Liam had a bad night. I think he's starting to teethe early, poor little mite.'

'That means you must've had a bad night too.' Evie held out the brown paper bag to her friend. 'I won't come too close but I've brought you these. Get them down you. I expect Dad's got some whisky if you want to make a hot toddy.'

Kate peered into the bag. 'I can't stand the taste of whisky, but thanks. Oh, for a couple of hours snuggling under the duvet! I love my little boy to pieces but babies are hard work sometimes.'

Evie thought quickly. Surely her sewing could wait an hour so?

'How about I take him for a walk? Unless he wants feeding or changing . . . or something?'

'Oh, would you really do that for me? He's actually all dressed up and in his pushchair. I was going to put my coat on and take him out when you arrived.'

'I'm glad I got here when I did because it's freezing out there, Kate. He looks very cosy but I'll keep the hood up to shield him.'

Within moments, Evie had wheeled Liam through to the front door and set off the way she came. It was challenging, tackling the slope, but the baby soon quietened down. When she dared pause to peep beneath the pushchair hood, Liam's eyelashes made dark fans on his rosy cheeks and he looked snug as a bug beneath the covers.

As the slope flattened out, Evie headed for the church, hoping she wouldn't bump into Jake. Her feelings were far too fragile after last night.

She wheeled her charge on until she came to the primary school and paused, hearing the sound of children's voices singing carols. Was this where Jake spent his early years? Had he dressed up as a shepherd in his first Nativity play? Maybe his teacher had noticed those eyelashes and given him the role of the angel!

She checked; the baby was still asleep. She didn't want to risk him waking, so she pushed him towards the church. She noticed Liam's top blanket had loosened and she was tucking it in when a car drove slowly past. When she glanced up, she realised it was Jake's vehicle.

This time, she could see what looked like straw bales pressing against the rear window. That seemed an unlikely cargo for an antiques dealer. But he'd obviously not noticed her, bent over the pram, and now he'd disappeared from sight.

It seemed impossible for her not to think about him. She really needed to pull herself together.

★   ★   ★

Rounding the curve in the road, Jake sucked in his breath. There she was, a sea-green woollen cap jammed over her tawny hair, bending over a pushchair. Evie actually had a baby.

He clenched his jaw and changed gear. It was understandable for their paths to keep crossing, given they lived in the same village, but must his whole system plunge into meltdown whenever he saw her?

There had been no sign of the baby's father last night. Maybe the guy was still in London and visited Evie and his son or daughter each weekend? That was plausible. If Evie's partner had let her know he was unable to visit that weekend, it could account for Jake having caught her in tears in her car. It seemed an age ago rather than only the Saturday before. The baby's grandmother must have been looking after the child, as Evie was definitely alone in the vehicle.

He hated to think of her being unhappy. What kind of a man must her partner be? Jake pulled in beside the churchyard railings and opened the boot. Hopefully the vicar would have unlocked the south door so he could deliver his straw bale.

Pining for someone so obviously taken was not only pointless but it hurt, because for the first time in years, he felt fully alive again. No longer numb.

And that, surely, must be a good sign.

As she neared the ancient church with its square tower displaying its Norman origins, Evie realised this was the perfect opportunity to call in. If it was locked, she'd return some other time but she wanted another couple of photos, from different angles, so she could plan the tableau for when her father delivered the figures.

She wasn't surprised to find the main entrance secured. Evie walked round the side of the building and found the south door ajar, so she pushed it wide, carefully manoeuvring the pushchair into the choir's robing room and closing the door behind her. She could hear the vicar talking to someone and walked through the curtained archway into the church, feeling a little awkward.

'Good morning, Vicar. Is it all right to take a few photographs to help me sketch out our tableau?'

The vicar greeted her. His companion was busy spreading straw around.

Evie's gaze fixed on his trim rear encased in a pair of taut black jeans and groaned inwardly. She might have known! How much torment could a girl take?

Jake peered over his shoulder. 'Am I in your way, Evie? We've almost done here.'

'I won't be long.' She pulled her phone from her pocket. But as she took the first shot, Jake appeared in the viewfinder. Flustered, she took the photo, moved and tried again.

'Jake kindly volunteered to collect straw from his farming friend so we could add an authentic touch,' explained the vicar.

'Really?' Evie moved again and aimed.

'Don't you like the idea?' Jake got to his feet.

Evie stared at him. 'I hadn't considered using straw, with all the sewing I've been doing.' She felt slightly miffed at not having been consulted.

Jake looked puzzled. 'Your father asked me last night if I had any farming contacts, because he thought spreading straw on the stone floor would add to the atmosphere.'

'Right.'

'So, if this was meant as a surprise, then it looks like you and I have just blown it.' He made a wry face.

Evie felt warmth flood her cheeks. She cleared her throat. 'I won't breathe a word when I get back then.' She suddenly remembered her manners. 'Thanks anyway for taking the trouble. I can see what Dad means now, but I just wish there was more time to do everything. I really want to make this into something special.'

'I'm sure you will, my dear.'

Evie had almost forgotten the vicar was still leaning on the pulpit, probably enjoying the show. Tension crackled in the air.

'Dad's almost finished with the figures and there's more sewing to do, but we hope to set up the tableau tomorrow. Will that be OK?'

A plaintive cry echoed from the choir

room. The vicar frowned and Evie looked stricken.

'Sorry about that! I brought Liam out for a walk and a nap but it sounds as though he's just woken up, so I'd better get him home again pronto.'

'Ah, you can't beat a walk in the fresh air.' The vicar consulted his watch. 'I'm due at the school soon so I'd best lock up now, if you two are done. Thanks again, Jake — and I'll see you and Charlie in the morning, Evie?'

She was conscious of Jake's presence behind her as she headed back to Kate's baby, who seemed to have settled back to sleep.

'Erm, looks like a grand little chap,' Jake said.

'I guess! I still have a lotto learn about babies.' Evie took the brake off the pram and turned it round to face the exit.

Jake leapt to open the door. 'Can I offer you a lift back?'

'That's very kind, but we'll be fine. I think he's gone back to sleep, thank goodness. He had a bad night so the longer he sleeps now, the better.'

'See you around, then.'

She pulled on her gloves. 'Yes, see you.'

★ ★ ★

Evie spent the rest of the morning working on the Holy Family's garments. She put one of her favourite music compilations on a loop and felt more relaxed as the day wore on. Her mother had gone into Elmchester on a mysterious errand and wasn't due back until later. Charlie Meredith was still putting final touches to the wooden figures.

Evie and her dad met at lunchtime where she found him in the kitchen, heating soup.

'Your mother's taken some goulash from the freezer for this evening, but I thought we could do with something warming to keep us going.'

'Lovely, Dad. It certainly is freezing

cold out there. I hope to finish my stuff this afternoon.'

'So if I take the figures down to St Stephen's tomorrow morning, you could come with me to see how the total effect looks?'

Evie couldn't resist teasing.

'You know what would be good, Dad? When I was in there this morning, I couldn't help thinking a layer of straw might be a good idea, to make the scene more realistic. Don't you think?'

Her dad began whistling as he stirred the soup.

'It's OK, I arrived just in time to see the straw being spread.' She took out her phone and called up her photos. 'See?'

'Well, I see a good shot of someone's rear end.' He sounded amused. 'But I hope you're pleased with the straw, Evie. Sorry, darling — I really should have run my idea by you first.'

Hurriedly, Evie stroked her finger across the screen to bring up the next shot. 'Jake happened to move as I was about to take the first photo. Seriously, Dad, I have to admit the straw's a good touch. I've brought my sketch pad in to show you how I see the tableau.'

'You know your stuff, Evie. I shan't argue with you. I did wonder if I was being cheeky, asking Jake to help but it seems like it's working out.'

Evie reached for the breadboard and the new loaf she'd brought back. 'Have the Vallances been in the village for ever, or are they incomers?'

'You'd best ask your mother, but I know his family moved here from London after his grandparents went into sheltered accommodation.'

'Was he grown up by then? Just wondering.'

'I believe he was at uni. Not sure if that denotes being grown up or not!'

'Very funny, Dad. So has Mr Vallance been running his emporium for long?'

'About five years, if I remember correctly. We've already been here the best part of a year, believe it or not.' He turned off the heat. 'This soup's ready to serve.'

'I'll get some cutlery. So, Jake must be a great help to his father? Being based in London, he must have loads of contacts?'

'You seem very interested in the young man, Evie. It's good that you're not bitter and twisted about that Marcus fellow. I realise it's none of my business, but I hated seeing you so unhappy. After only a few days with us, I can see a change in you. And I don't for one minute think it's down to those hours spent at the sewing machine!'

6

Next morning Evie placed the suitcase containing her finished work on the back seat of her dad's car then hopped into the passenger seat. Stray snow-flakes drifted down from a grim grey sky.

Her father was in the driving seat, peering heavenwards. 'There's more to come, by the looks. And the forecast wasn't good this morning.'

'We'll soon have the tableau in position, though I'll need time to add some little touches.'

'Your mother wants me to go along and put lights up for a pair of eighty-something sisters when I finish here. I can always come back for you if the snow settles.'

'Don't worry about me, Dad. I'll get down that slope somehow.'

'Well, take it steady and come down

the grassy side if necessary. But I expect you'll be glad of some peace to do your fiddly bits in the church.'

Evie gazed out of the window as her father drove. 'I still can't get over how quiet it is, with the children in school and hardly any vehicles.'

'It's one of the reasons why we chose Mossford.'

Soon they were passing the village green. A little further along from the pub, the Vallance residence loomed into view. Evie averted her gaze. So far that morning she'd managed not to conjure up Jake in her mind's eye.

It was a relief to begin unloading the figures. The vicar had made the south entrance available and Evie entered the tranquil interior, to carry out a final check of the straw-covered flagstones before her father positioned the crib. She'd created a star to suspend so one of the spotlights could be focused on it and make it appear to twinkle. She'd also made gifts to pile beside the manger, using her imagination plus research into the frankincense, gold and myrrh offerings. While the church was open to visitors, there would be soft music playing — newer tunes as well as traditional carols. The vicar and his wife had readily agreed to switch the music on and off and Evie felt surprisingly upbeat about the whole enterprise.

Once the figures were in place, she began slipping the garments on to each of them. Her father placed the babe, already bundled up in swaddling clothes, into the manger.

'Looking good, Dad.' Evie stood, hands on hips, surveying their handiwork. 'It's so much better than before, yet without being too flashy.'

Her father moved back a few pews.

'Needs something to perk it up, but I imagine that's what you're about to do.'

Evie produced her star from a carrier bag. 'How about this? I'll need your help to get it into position. It needs to be in line with that spotlight.'

'I'll borrow the stepladder from the back room and attach the star . . . just there, do you reckon?' He pointed to one of the columns.

'That should do well.'

It took a while before Evie was satisfied with the effect and her father could leave.

'You do realise one school of thought believes the three wise men were following the trail of a comet?' Charlie folded up the ladder.

'That's interesting, Dad. I think we'll stay with the Star of Bethlehem, thanks.'

Left alone, Evie took more photographs. Scrolling through, she reached the one where Jake had stepped into her camera's viewfinder and for moments she stared at his image, feeling her pulse race a little faster. How sad was that? She put away her phone and stood, wondering what else would make the scene more realistic.

A movement by the choir stalls startled her.

'Hello? Is anyone there?' Her throat constricted. You never knew if you were totally safe anywhere these days, even in a village church.

'Hi, Evie, it's only me.' A figure emerged. 'I didn't mean to make you jump. I'm on my way to Elmchester and thought I'd call in to see how you and Charlie were getting on.'

She pulled herself together. Cleared her throat. 'Sorry, but you've just missed him, I'm afraid. Was there anything special? I'm wondering what else I can add. I was thinking about flowers but I haven't a clue what I could use and I don't want to spoil the natural effect. I've never worked on a religious theme before ... ' *Stop gabbling, Evie!*

Jake was closer now. He wore a navy polo neck with an old, good quality duffle coat over dark jeans. He smelled like a pine forest in the evening, after sunlight had sweet-talked the trees.

Evie stuck both hands into the pockets of her dove-grey, puffy jacket and felt her nails bite into her palms. *Concentrate, woman! Remember you're single and you've decided it's best to keep it that way.*

Jake gave a long, low whistle and turned to her. 'You've done a great job.'

'Dad did all the difficult stuff.'

'He'd probably say otherwise. Who painted the faces?'

'That'd be me.'

'They're amazing. How about the clothes?'

'Guilty again.'

'The pair of you obviously make a good team. I'm just thinking, back in our store room there's a battered old milk churn, nothing too large, but it might just add that extra touch and you're very welcome to borrow it.'

She turned to face him. If she stood on tiptoe and placed one hand on each of his broad shoulders, she'd only have to lean towards him and their mouths would . . .

'Evie,' he said, huskily. 'I have to know. Is there someone special in your life or are you single? It's none of my business, but I can't help wondering about your baby's father.'

'My. Baby's. Father?' *I sound like. Lady Bracknell in The Importance of Being Ernest when she makes her famous handbag comment.*

He stepped closer. 'Forgive me if I'm out of order. I . . . you . . . oh, hell's bells! Evie, I can't stop thinking about you. So if you want me to back off, you'd better tell me now before I take you in my arms and kiss you senseless!' He looked towards the altar, his expression rueful. 'I'm so sorry if you're up there listening to this, but I am only human after all.'

First of all, Evie wanted to laugh. Then she wanted to jump for joy. This man was delightful. And funny. She closed her eyes for a moment. And boy, even if she was in church, she had to acknowledge he was hot! But what made him think she was a mother?

'Evie? I didn't see the pushchair on my way in and I thought I'd better check the situation before I take the plunge and ask you out.'

Light dawned. 'Ah — you think Wills and Kate's baby belongs to me?'

'I know Wills is a proud dad, but are you saying the baby with you yesterday isn't yours?'

'I volunteered to take Liam for a walk as his mum was feeling poorly.'

He frowned. 'Now, hang on! At the meeting on Monday, I distinctly heard you say you were going to check on your baby.'

Now she could allow herself to laugh and release some of the tension inside her.

'You heard right, but I was referring to my red setter, Rusty. The one thing making life bearable at the moment is my adorable little dog.'

Jake raised a hand and stroked her cheek. His fingers felt warm.

I think my legs are about to dissolve beneath me . . .

'I keep thinking how I found you in tears. You're obviously distraught over something. Whatever's going on, I wish I could put it right for you.'

Careful, Evie. Can your poor, broken heart really mend so quickly? If you tell Jake you can't stop thinking about him either, you'll be on a slippery slope to the roller-coaster ride of your life!

Her feet couldn't move, even if she wanted them to. His mouth was a heartbeat away from hers. The kiss she hadn't been able to stop fantasising about was about to happen. How could she possibly resist?

The ringing of her phone broke the magic.

'You'd better get that.' Jake spoke softly and backed away.

Evie kept her eyes on him but accepted the call. 'What is it, Dad?'

He wasted no time in telling her. Offered to collect her from the church.

'You're joking! I can't bear the thought of setting eyes on him!' she hissed down the phone. 'Tell him to get back to London where he belongs.' She shot a frantic look at Jake, staring at his feet, arms folded. A muscle twitched in his right cheek.

Her father wouldn't listen.

'Evie, the man's driven from London. At least let him say what he obviously wants to say to you. I'll get the coffee going and I'll drive you back to the church afterwards if you want.'

She closed the call and looked at Jake.

'My ex has turned up and my father insists I speak to him. It's my parents' home and I can't order Dad to boot him out.'

'I understand. I'll drop you off on my way to Elmchester.'

'But we're not exactly on your route.'

'Evie, the sooner you get back and deal with what's obviously a difficult situation, the better. Come on!'

She followed him out. She'd need to ring the vicar later and apologise for rushing off. The earlier sprinkling of snow had vanished but sullen grey clouds hung low in the sky and the wind was making tree branches sway.

Jake zapped his key and opened the

96

passenger door. Taking his place beside her, he patted her hand. 'Maybe some things aren't meant to be.'

Evie struggled to speak. One look at his profile told her he was distancing himself. But that was what she'd decided was best, wasn't it?

He pulled up outside her parents' gate and turned to her. 'You know where I am, Evie.'

She nodded. 'This isn't what I expected. I'm so sorry, Jake.'

'Not half as sorry as I am, but I'm not about to complicate your life any more than it is already. Take care. Be sure to tell your father to stay within earshot. Oh, and I'll bring that churn later.'

She croaked her thanks, then got out and hurried round to the back door, afraid if she lingered, she'd be begging him to take her to Elmchester with him. But what would be the point? Marcus had the determination of a thundering rhinoceros once he made up his mind about something. He'd hang around, waiting until she returned, meaning her father would be upset and inconvenienced. It was a pity her mum wasn't at home. Helen would have seen him off, that was for sure. Anyway, this would be the first time Marcus would find himself unable to bend Evie's will to his.

In the kitchen her ex-boyfriend, wearing a black cashmere sweater over dark grey cords, sat opposite her father at the scrubbed pine table. Evie began unbuttoning her jacket.

'Darling, you look fabulous! Country air obviously suits you.' Marcus got up from his chair. He'd probably spent a three-figure sum on having his blond hair cut.

'You're only staying for coffee because my father's being polite, Marcus. You wouldn't have got beyond the front door if I'd had my way.'

She turned her head abruptly so that his kiss landed on her ear. She moved over to the shiny dark blue kitchen range, leaning against the rail and feeling the welcome warmth against her body.

Her father cleared his throat.

'Coffee's ready to pour. I'm going to leave you two to talk so I'll take mine into the study.' He paused. 'Oh, and, um, Marcus has brought you a bouquet. I've stood the flowers in the washing-up bowl for now.'

Evie still didn't speak.

'Thanks, Charlie.' Marcus injected just the right amount of humility into his comment. It was as if he was bonding with her father — humouring her, the only one who hadn't read the script.

'Coffee? And your father's put out your favourite biscuits, I see.'

'No coffee. Explain why you're here, then go.'

Marcus sighed and sat down again. 'I understand why you're furious with me, darling.'

'Really? Well, how extremely clever of you!'

'You look beautiful when you're

angry. I've never seen you so wound up. It's rather exciting.'

She looked him in the eyes. He shrugged.

'It's life, sweetie. Full of ups and downs. We had a fabulous whirl. Then it was time to part.'

'Correction. You decided to dump me.'

He shook his head. 'Such a horrendous expression. Our relationship had reached a point where we both knew it wasn't working.'

'You may be many things, Marcus, but you're not a mind reader. However, I realise I should be grateful to be out of your clutches and able to get on with the rest of my life.'

He smiled. That sad, little-boy-lost smile that no longer had any effect. She looked at her watch.

'Do you have another appointment, darling? Your father told me you've been joining in with village events. It all sounds so quaint and jolly.'

'Marcus, don't let me keep you.'

'I want you to come back to London with me, Evie. Today.'

'You must be joking!'

'Believe me, what I'm about to tell you will have you gagging to fly away with me. It's the opportunity of a lifetime, darling. Please, please, let me explain to you what it's all about.'

* * *

Jake parked in the yard behind his father's shop. On the drive from Mossford he'd tried his best to concentrate on his day's schedule but now he sat still, his mind replaying the scene in the church. He'd been so close to kissing Evie. And he knew he wouldn't have received a rejection. Suspecting her fragility, he'd been on the verge of asking permission, even though the dreamy expression on her face and the tenderness in her eyes were so heartening.

Then the phone call shattered the mood. She obviously hadn't wanted to leave but he knew she must. He hadn't seen Evie's eyes blaze like that before and he wondered what her unexpected visitor had done to cause such a strong reaction.

Could Evie be his second chance of finding happiness? He'd found it the first time with Lacy, the beautiful American girl he met at university. They'd been inseparable for a few years, then had a tremendous bust-up when she wanted him to accompany her on a skiing holiday. He'd hated the idea and wouldn't even consider it. In the end she contacted a girlfriend still living in the States who agreed to accompany her.

Jake had realised the closeness between him and Lacy was over. She flew to Canada and on the third day at the ski resort, must have ignored the warning flags or been distracted, because she'd wandered off piste and into the path of an avalanche. It must have been terrifying and he still sometimes had bad dreams, waking up imagining how she would have felt. The search team found her too late.

Jake, devastated, had been consumed with guilt for two years until his father took him aside and convinced him Lacy wouldn't want him to wear a hair shirt for the rest of his life.

Now at last, another young woman had sparked a feeling within him, making him wonder if it was time to trust his emotions and set about winning Evie's heart. But she seemed elusive. He could understand her frostiness on their first meeting, but each time they'd been thrown together since, she seemed to have warmed towards him, especially when he revealed how he'd been convinced she was a mother.

The delicious sound of her laugh still rang in his ears, yet Charlie's phone call wasn't only bad timing, it was the warning bell for the barriers to come up again. And now, at this very moment, her former partner — who had to be an idiot to let her go in the first place

— might be on his knees, begging Evie's forgiveness, maybe even opening up a jewellery box . . .

7

'You must remember Damian and Larissa? Of course you do! He's the one whose pa owns all that New York real estate. They've got free run of a villa on the family's private island for three weeks. We fly from Heathrow the week before Christmas, night-stop, then take a helicopter to paradise.'

He waved his phone. 'Take a look at how fabulous the island is.'

Evie shook her head. 'No way.'

'The sand's a pale gold. The ocean looks jade green, or turquoise blue, depending on the light. There are palm trees and flamingos. We can swim and scuba dive with no having to shop or cook because there are staff to do our bidding.'

'I can imagine. I feel sorry for those unfortunate islanders, having to wait on an arrogant man like you. I can't believe how blind I was!'

'All in the past. Please be my Plus One, darling. Believe me, that girl didn't mean anything to me! I made a foolish mistake. I'm sorry if I hurt you.'

'Hurt me? You made a laughing stock of me, Marcus. Even that McDonnell-Brown woman heard about it.'

He raised his eyebrows. 'Melissa? How interesting! I didn't know you were chums with Mel.'

'That's because I'm not! Another of your old flames, isn't she? And how convenient that she has a second home in this village. Here's an idea! Why don't you call round? I'm sure she'd give you a really warm welcome.'

Marcus chuckled. 'How you've changed! I love the way you fight back at me. I know you can't wait to give me the answer I want, so why don't you come sit on my knee so I can whisper naughty nothings in your ear while your dad's not listening? Then you really must pack that big wheelie case of yours. The weather will be lovely and I've never seen you in a bikini.' His eyes travelled over her body, as if he was considering purchasing a new sports car.

A wave of fury hit her. She darted over to the sink, grabbed not only the huge bouquet but the washing up bowl too, and while Marcus was checking his phone, she dumped both flowers and water over him.

In the stunned silence following, she felt hugely triumphant. For moments he sat, open-mouthed, one single crimson rose lodged behind his right ear.

'My cashmere sweater!' Marcus yelled. 'And my phone! How could you be so thoughtless? I don't have any spare clothes with me.'

'Then you'd better drive back to London and find some. Now, while the roads are still clear.'

'Everything all right?' Evie's father popped his head round the door. His jaw dropped on noticing the decidedly soggy guest. 'Oh, dear.'

'It's all right, Dad. Our visitor isn't

staying.' Evie reached into a cupboard and took out a kitchen roll. She threw it to Marcus. 'Keep it.'

'I'm not leaving without you, Evie. Even if you insist on behaving like a spoilt child.'

'Excuse me, young man.' Charlie walked up to Marcus who was dabbing at himself with a wad of paper towels. 'I think you'd best go now. Evie isn't going to change her mind.'

Evie sucked in her breath. Marcus looked at her, looked back at her father and nodded.

'You're making a big mistake, you silly girl. Weren't you hoping to get a contract for that new show in January? You know, the job you said you really fancied . . . ' His mouth twisted.

'Please don't threaten my daughter, Marcus. You broke her heart once. Don't push your luck or I'll report you for intimidating behaviour.'

Marcus rammed his phone in his pocket and picked up his keys.

'I'll fetch your coat.' Evie's dad,

looking relieved, opened the door wide and hurried out.

'I shan't argue with an old man.' Marcus spoke menacingly. 'But believe it, no way will I forget what you did. Watch your back, darling.'

As he strutted out, Evie felt only relief.

★　★　★

Evie glanced at the scene outside the sitting room window. 'Good job you came back when you did, Mum. The snow's well and truly settling.'

'It's so pretty but such a total pain. I was stocking up with festive goodies from the farm shop when it started and I didn't hang around. So, did you manage to finish your tableau?'

'You bet. When I went back, the vicar seemed pleased, so that's something.'

'Marcus must be on the motorway by now. You wouldn't want him being stranded in the village, would you, poor love?'

'I really don't want to talk about him, Mum. Dad's brought you up to date, hasn't he?'

'The moment I walked in the door. You'd already gone back to the church, of course. I can't remember when I last saw your father so angry.'

'Oh, he was amazing, the way he put Marcus in his place. But how I could ever have imagined I was in love with that scumbag beats me.'

Helen shrugged. 'We all make mistakes. He had a nerve, though, turning up unannounced and expecting you to swoon into his arms.'

Evie hid a smile. Her mum enjoyed reading a particular style of romantic novel. But she couldn't get her mind off Jake, who'd been heading for Elmchester. Was he aware how relentlessly the snow was falling in Mossford? With Mr Vallance's back still so painful, he might not realise the road home could make travelling difficult for his son, and she'd no idea where Mrs Vallance might be.

'Mum, do you have Jake's mobile number?'

Her mother gave her an odd look.

'I don't, I'm afraid. You'll find the Vallances' landline number in the book on the hall table. Or you can look up the shop number online.'

'Of course. Thanks, Mum. Jake brought me back from the church this morning and he said he was going to the emporium. I think I might ring and check if he's aware of the weather situation.'

'Whatever you think best.' She gave Evie a searching look. 'Something you want to tell me?'

Evie shook her head. What passed between her and Jake earlier in the church was still too recent, too poignant, to discuss, even with her mum. But she didn't want to hurt Jake, and she thought he deserved an explanation as to why Marcus turned up so unexpectedly.

That awful visit from her ex had totally convinced her how lucky an escape she'd had. But she needed to get her emotions under control. This attraction to Jake couldn't be allowed to grow.

Somehow I must harden my heart. It's far too soon even to think of another relationship. But if only my body would acknowledge what my brain knows.

'Jake's a nice guy, Mum. I know he's only around for a few weeks, but the same goes for me. No reason why we can't be friends.'

'No reason at all.' Her mother turned away, and Evie got the feeling she was hiding a smirk.

Evie sat down and opened her laptop. Moments later she found the Vallance Emporium's number, jotted it down and went straight to the hall.

A woman's voice answered and Evie asked for Jake. 'It's Evie Meredith. I'm a friend of his.'

'He's busy with a customer at the moment. Would you like him to ring you back?'

'Yes, that'd be good. Thank you.'

She left her mobile phone number and rang off, feeling foolish. Why hadn't she asked the assistant to take a message? Jake might be ages with the customer. There might not even be much snow in Elmchester — if any.

She could hear her mum on the phone in the hallway. At this rate, any normal woman would be dangerously close to burnout by Christmas. But this was Superwoman! At least, with the tableau in position and only the music to be sorted out, she was taking some of the festive preparations off her mum's hands.

Evie returned to her laptop and began researching websites connected to her set decorator job. Her mother had gone upstairs. Evie became engrossed and sent a couple of emails, feeling it might be a good idea not to put all her hopes on the job in Switzerland. Marcus didn't frighten her, but if he really did turn spiteful, he'd be capable of badmouthing her among certain of his cronies.

She jumped when the landline rang and hoped it was Jake calling. The second, far less attractive option was that it might be Marcus. She'd just got up when the ringing stopped; her mother must have taken the call upstairs. Sure enough, she heard her name being called so hurtled out into the hallway.

'Is that for me?'

'Yes, darling. Pick up, I'll put this one down.'

Evie felt all fingers and thumbs but managed not to cut the caller off.

'Thanks for ringing back,' she said.

'Are you all right? I didn't like to ask your mother.'

'Fine, thanks. My visitor had a cup of coffee and set off back to London.'

'Well, as long as you're OK.'

He sounds so concerned . . .

'So, what can I do for you, Evie? I've put the churn in my car, by the way.'

'Thanks, but this isn't about the churn. I wondered whether you knew what road conditions are like between Elmchester and here.'

'We've had a light sprinkling — hang on while I take a look. I'm just walking through to the showroom.' He paused. 'Ah. Actually it's a lot heavier than it was. What's it like in the village?'

'It's been snowing heavily for a couple of hours. I thought I'd better warn you, because I've looked online and there's no gritting been done in these parts, so people are advised to play safe and get back home while they can.'

'Evie, thanks for thinking of me, but my vehicle has four-wheel drive so I shall finish what I need to do and make a decision in another hour or so.'

She bit her lip. She hadn't taken his vehicle into account and as he lived on the village's upper level, he'd probably be fine.

'Well, have a safe journey and, um, well, I'll see you around, I guess.'

Well done, Evie! You need to give yourself space to think. Your poor old heart's taken a battering. You've made the right decision. Harden it and don't be in a hurry to fall in love again.

'I'll give you a call when I've delivered the churn to the church. Take care.'

She put the phone down. He was at the antiques shop and he was in business mode. But she wondered what might have happened had Marcus not turned up and caused her dad to make that phone call.

★   ★   ★

So Evie was thinking about him? Jake resisted the impulse to punch the air. The cold feeling of dread enveloping him once he discovered her ex-boyfriend had driven from London was a significant reminder of just how much she'd slipped beneath his radar, jolting him into realising how he'd been avoiding a new romance.

But he couldn't forget that picture of her, hunched over the steering wheel

116

and crying her heart out. No way could he blame her if she decided to stay out of the dating game for a while.

Churches were tinderboxes of emotion. Brides and grooms had been known to dissolve into giggles when the other fluffed their vows. Being jilted at the altar, attending church to say a final goodbye to a loved one, seeing someone unexpected walk in . . . the atmosphere must be a powerful blend of tears, love, regrets, doubts and broken promises.

It was clear how much effort Evie had put into creating that Nativity tableau. When he'd complimented her, she was probably on a high, which would account for the stars in her eyes and the roses in her cheeks. No. He'd made a mistake. It wasn't right to pester the poor girl. Just as he had done for so long, she'd probably put up a protective barrier, and he must respect that decision and not try to melt Evie's heart.

★   ★   ★

Jake's assistant put her head round his office door on her return from lunch. 'It's like a wilderness out there, Jake. I'm wondering whether it's worth keeping open in such dreadful weather. They're forecasting widespread heavy snow for Gloucestershire and surrounding counties.'

'Yeah, the friend who rang sounded concerned. You should go home, Susie. I'll hang on a bit longer if you're OK to walk?'

'I'm fine, thanks. I always keep a pair of wellies here — I've been caught before!'

'You get off home then and I'll put a notice on the door. You're right — we're hardly likely to get a coachload of tourists in these conditions.'

Jake closed down his laptop. He called goodbye to Susie when she left, and did his security routine. Last of all, he locked the shop door, pushed his hood up over his dark hair and headed to his car. The odd vehicle drove slowly down the road as he scrunched through the snow. His own was barely visible beneath a fluffy white cocoon.

Having cleared the roof and windows, he took it very steadily through the town and on to the main road. On arrival in Mossford, he drove along the village street with a sense of relief. It had stopped snowing, but as he drew near the beautiful honey stone cottage owned by Melissa, a man getting something out of a red sports car caught his attention. The guy had obviously tried to manoeuvre his vehicle into the driveway but failed because of the huge snowdrift. Was this Melissa's new boyfriend, the American she'd talked about after the pub quiz? He'd been lucky to make it to the village in these conditions.

Jake reached home and parked in his own drive. His parents each had a car but they were inside the big double garage. He sat for a while after he switched off the engine, picturing Evie. He had no intention of trudging to the church with the churn now, but tomorrow he'd deliver it.

After all, he had promised to call her. And not to do so would be extremely rude.

★ ★ ★

Evie and her parents were watching the local television news.

'All those stranded vehicles! How awful for those poor people, having to abandon their cars,' Helen said.

'I wonder if his nibs is still on the road.' Evie's dad shook his head. 'I can't stand the fellow, but I wouldn't wish him any harm.'

'If I know Marcus, he'll have stopped at a pub or a hotel by now and will be propping up the bar.' Evie saw her parents exchange glances. 'No, I don't want to check he's all right. I didn't ask him to come here, did I?'

'Of course not,' her mother said. 'We couldn't do anything, anyway. I expect you're right and he's miles away by now, drowning his sorrows.'

But Evie's thoughts had drifted back to Jake. How would she be feeling now, if only their quiet time in the church hadn't been interrupted?

8

Jake was up early next morning, clearing a walkway from the front door. There'd been another fall in the night and the snow was soft so he worked quickly, banking it up either side.

The road through the village being cleared by a local farmer. Jake gave him a wave as he passed.

Inside the house, his mother was making breakfast and his father was already downstairs.

'You look a lot better today, Pa.' Jake hung his soggy gloves on the rail of the Raeburn and rubbed his freezing cold hands together.

'I feel much better. Yesterday I was wondering about going into the shop but that's not going to happen, is it?'

'Susie said she'd open up as long as she could walk into town. We don't want to miss out on trade if people are out and about.'

'No, indeed. Not when this month is peak time for our jewellery sales.'

'Be thankful your back's much better and give it a few more days at home — I would,' Jake's mother called out over the sound of eggs frying.

Jake turned up the radio volume. 'Time for the news. When they get to the local stuff we can find out more about the weather conditions. I'll make the toast, Ma, shall I?'

The news announcer gave information about road closures, lorries jack-knifing and blocking the nearest motorway, and a young mother who'd gone into labour and needed to be helicoptered to a maternity unit.

'Wow.' Jake sipped his coffee. 'Sounds as if it's been quite a night.'

He pulled a face on hearing the weather presenter talk about plummeting temperatures across the United Kingdom, making already difficult conditions even more treacherous. He switched off the radio as the broadcast ended.

'I haven't heard from Susie so hopefully she's opening up the shop today. I'll need to check before setting off.'

His father nodded. 'No point getting stuck.'

'Now you're making me wonder about our elderly folk, particularly at Lower Mossford.' Fleetingly he thought of Evie, knocking on doors to check people were all right.

His mother must have read his mind. 'I'll give Helen Meredith a ring in a while. See whether those slopes are passable.'

Jake hesitated. 'I'll hang on if you like.'

'Checking on people living alone would be a thoughtful thing to do,' his father said. 'This is the first time since you were a child that we've had such a bad snowfall. But don't try driving out of the village just yet.'

Jake shrugged. 'You've had more experience than I have. I promised to drop off something at the church but I can walk down there.'

'Unless it's absolutely vital, I'd leave it here for now. What if you slip and sprain your ankle?'

'I'm twenty-seven, not seventy-seven, Pa!'

'I'm not joking — it's treacherous out there, my boy. There's freezing fog forecast for later so you wouldn't want to hang around in town after mid-afternoon. You might regret it.'

⋆ ⋆ ⋆

'The weather's playing havoc with our pantomime rehearsals. It's at times like this I regret buying a house down here!' Evie's mum was prowling the sitting room like a caged lioness.

'Come on, it doesn't happen often,' Evie's dad said. 'We enjoy more peace and quiet than many folk do, so why fret over a bit of inconvenience once in a blue moon?'

Evie grinned. 'I'm going to try and

get to the church on foot, Mum. Do you need anything from the shop? I take it they'll be open?'

'I'm sure they will. I'm due there for the afternoon shift so all being well, I can bring back any bits and bobs then — thanks, Evie.'

'OK. It should be fun, clambering up the road. Good exercise, anyway. And I need to ring the vicarage because I want to put the final touches to the wise men. A few bits of bling should do the trick.'

Jake hasn't rung. Maybe he stayed the night in Elmchester. It would be good to know he's all right, though . . .

Outside, she found her car transformed into a thick white cocoon. Her mobile rang as she was walking gingerly up the path her father had cleared earlier. She stopped at the gate, sucking in her breath when she saw who was calling.

'How are you doing?' Jake sounded cautious.

'I'm just setting off but I think it'll

take me a while to fight my way up from the depths.' Her breath was making white puffs in the still, cold air. 'My mother seems to think living in Lower Mossford's like inhabiting Middle Earth.'

'Well, I'd offer to come and collect you but my father is convinced that should I leave the main highway, I shall never be seen again.'

Evie giggled. A warm feeling was spreading through her that had nothing to do with the fleece she wore beneath her bulky jacket. At that moment, the thought of being marooned with Jake in a cosy little cottage like the one where her friend Kate and Wills lived sounded very tempting.

But Jake was only being friendly. And never in a million years would she and he ever be living anywhere together, cosy cottage or otherwise.

'I sometimes think my parents imagine I revert to being a twelve-year-old the moment I walk in the door,' she said.

'Tell me about it! But I have to say, the old fella knows his village and the weather better than I do, and it would be pointless, not to mention embarrassing, if I got myself stuck and had to ring my farming mate to haul me out.'

'Not good for your man-about-town image.'

He was laughing again. She steeled herself.

This isn't the time for going weak at the knees, Evie. Will you never learn?

'I'm calling to confess I haven't been in touch with the vicar so the churn's still in our hallway.'

'Is it all right if I call and collect it, then? He's promised to open up the south door for me.'

'I feel as though I've let you down, Evie.'

'Absolutely not. I'm very grateful for the loan.'

'I'll call in and take a look at your Nativity scene as soon as I can.'

'Be warned! One of the Wise Men looks as if he's wearing mascara. Think

Captain Jack in *Pirates Of The Caribbean*, but apart from that, the tableau shouldn't look too bad.'

Jake was chuckling again. 'I can hardly wait.' He paused. 'I might just bump into you. My folks and I were talking about villagers who might need things from the shop. I do have a good mate who'd bring his tractor if necessary.'

'Would it help if I asked Mum to tell me who I should check on, then get back to you?'

'Evie, you're a star. That would be a tremendous help. Mind how you go though, dear.'

She grinned. 'I'll be in touch.'

Evie pushed her phone back in her pocket, his voice lingering in her ear. Why on earth couldn't she have met Jake in London last spring, instead of getting involved with dodgy Marcus? Here he was, giving up his time to help others less mobile.

'I never realised what a nice young man Jake Vallance is,' Helen said when she heard of the plan.

Evie soon knew the house numbers of three people who might appreciate a call. Then, wrapped up like an Eskimo, she set off, having decided to call on Kate first, even though Wills must have a vehicle suited to adverse conditions. Looking back, she saw her boots had made neat prints in the pristine surface, with no sign of anyone else having passed by, except for some inquisitive cat.

When she reached her friends' cottage, she saw what she imagined must be Wills' Land Rover beneath a thick white blanket and the path to the door was still buried. It took her a while to get the gate open, as she had to kick away sufficient snow to allow her to squeeze through.

Kate came to the door quickly, the baby asleep in her arms.

'Come in, Evie. Lovely to see you! I don't think I'm harbouring any germs, but Wills is down with the lurgy now. I ordered him to stay in bed and when he didn't complain, I knew he must be feeling rough.'

'I won't come any further, thanks. Is there a shovel handy, so I can clear your path?'

'If you're not short of time, you could come in and keep an eye on Liam while I clear it.'

'Oh, I'm sure he'd far rather have his mummy with him,' Evie said hastily. 'I can babysit him some other time though, if you fancy a break.'

'You're an angel, Evie. Wills left a shovel inside the back door so I'll get it for you. I do feel guilty.'

'Well, don't! The exercise will be good for me.'

Evie felt a sense of satisfaction after clearing a track through the drifts either side of the gate. She gave her friend a knock and asked if Kate needed anything from the shop.

'Gosh, yes, I could do with baby milk, please. Whoever's on duty will know the kind I get. And they were getting some baby rusks in.'

'Do you have painkillers for Wills? And how about a couple of lemons if they have them?'

'You're thinking more clearly than me. We pay our account weekly, they'll just add what you buy.'

'Sure that's all you need?'

'I always keep the freezer well-stocked, but thanks, Evie.'

Evie set off again, collecting two more orders from grateful people and sending Jake a text message. When the road began to climb, she moved on to the grassy verge. At least, if she took a tumble here, she shouldn't come to much harm. At last she was at the top and walking along still-pristine pavements.

She and the vicar's wife were putting goods into bags when Evie heard the sounds of someone knocking snow off their boots. The shop bell clanged and Jake arrived, bringing a cloud of frosty air with him.

'Morning, ladies. Evie, I've got Farmer Freddie waiting outside on his tractor. He's going to clear a passage-way down to your neck of the woods, then drive through and up the other slope. If you're ready, we can take the shopping — give you a lift if you want.'

Evie thought quickly. Maybe she'd be wiser not spending too much time with Jake.

He began hooking shopping bags over one arm. 'Evie? Or are you going walkabout?'

'I really want to take photographs inside the church, but thanks so much for your help. I'll see you at the next rehearsal.'

He nodded. Evie felt a pang as he left, but tried to keep her mind occupied. She set off again, taking a few photos with her phone as she walked through the village. She had a friend out in Australia who'd enjoy the picturesque snow scenes. She called at the Vallances' house and Jake's father showed her where the churn, which fortunately wasn't too large, stood ready.

At the church, snow clearance was still in progress and she was grateful to walk around to the rear and kick off her wellies, walking through to the nave in thick woolly socks.

After adding her finishing touches to the Wise Men and putting the churn in position, she took more photographs, capturing the tableau from several angles.

Evie went to say goodbye to the vicar.

'I'll check it out in a while, Evie, but you and Charlie have done a great job. I can't thank you enough. Let's hope the snow doesn't stop folk from coming to church tomorrow.'

On the way back to the shop, Evie noticed a couple walking ahead, the woman dressed in a long red fox-fur coat and matching hat, looking as if she was starring in *Dr Zhivago*. She was clinging to the arm of a man wearing an overcoat that belonged in one of London's fashionable arcades rather than a village street. He had blond hair and, as he turned to say something,

Evie realised who it was. Her heart almost stopped in shock. Marcus was still in the village, and clearly enjoying the company of the woman snuggled against him — Melissa McDonnell-Brown.

Her imagination in overdrive, Evie slowed down and prayed her ex didn't turn round. So he hadn't even attempted to leave the village? The scheming, good-for-nothing waster obviously possessed Melissa's phone number and, not wanting to face a potential snowstorm, had thrown himself on her mercy.

Evie wondered how the unexpected guest would go down with Melissa's American beau when he eventually arrived in Mossford. She aimed her phone camera at a particularly lovely holly bush. Someone must have given it a shake because clusters of bright berries poked out of the snow, making a real-life Christmas card scene.

Please let Marcus and Melissa be heading for the pub, not the shop! It was a little early to be drinking but he'd never let that get in his way before. Much to her relief, the couple stopped outside The Wheatsheaf and knocked snow from their boots. He must have said something to amuse Melissa because she looked up at him, laughing, before he opened the door and they disappeared without a backward glance.

Evie trudged towards home, thankful when she could edge down the snowy slope, trying not to feel anxious because her ex was still around.

★   ★   ★

'It seems Marcus never even got as far as the main road yesterday.' Evie hung up her jacket.

'Has he been in touch? Did he sleep in his car? I don't think he'd have been the only one!' her mother exclaimed.

'He hasn't contacted me, thank goodness. I saw him in the village with Melissa but luckily I was behind them.' Evie unwound her lime-green scarf. 'Jake and his friend have done a grand job. I left them to it and went to the church.'

Evie went into the kitchen, still fuming over her ex. 'Marcus obviously has Melissa's mobile number. I have a feeling they were once an item.'

Her mother's mobile phone buzzed.

'Someone's texting you, Mum,' Evie called.

Helen hurried in. 'I hope no one's pulling out of the pantomime. We've already had one person decide she didn't want to freeze to death in the village hall in a flimsy frock!' She sniffed. 'Luckily, Melissa McDonnell-Brown's housekeeper has agreed to be our fairy godmother.'

'I could do with one of those,' Evie murmured.

Meanwhile, her mother checked the text, then groaned. 'Oh, I don't believe this!'

'What's up?' Evie was still fuming over Marcus.

Her mother was making a phone call now, using the landline. Evie, desperate for a hot drink, was mixing two instant coffees and wondering what Marcus' plan was. Surely he didn't intend to steal his old flame away before her new boyfriend arrived? Could Melissa be that stupid?

Helen bustled back and picked up her mug.

'Thanks, Evie. I sometimes wonder whether this pantomime is worth the hassle.'

'Sit down, Mum, and tell me what's happened.'

'You couldn't make it up! Our Prince Charming and our Cinderella, played by a lovely young engaged couple, have had the most enormous row. Her mother says she's broken off the engagement and no way will she take part in the panto now, even if we found another prince.'

'Might it only be a case of pre-wedding jitters?'

Her mother sighed. 'I wish! It seems Prince Charming was also having a relationship with someone from work.

Due to the snow, he got marooned at this other girl's flat in Elmchester and rang to tell his fiancee he was staying with an office colleague. But the friend whose name he gave posted a message on Chatbook or whatever it is, asking if Prince Charming had got home all right. Cinderella saw it; you can guess the rest.'

Evie could. 'So when's the panto taking place?'

'We start the day after Boxing Day, so it's three evening shows with a Saturday matinee. The villagers love their panto and always bring in friends and family from round and about. Somehow, we've got to find a way out of this.'

Evie thought her mother was about to burst into tears, until she saw the expression on her face.

'I've got it! You can take over the role, darling.'

'Oh no, Mother! No. No. No. Believe me, there is no way I'm taking this on.'

'But you've finished the tableau. Speaking of which, the vicar's posted some photos on the village website. You're very creative, darling. I'm so proud of you and your father for helping out.'

'Thanks, Mum, but don't change the subject.'

'I was about to say the script is good and you're about the same size as our original Cinders. There's only the ragged dress and the ballgown to alter — and you're the perfect person to make any changes, now, aren't you?'

Evie drank some coffee. 'You must promote someone who's already in the cast and I'll think — only think, mind you — about taking on that person's role, as long as it's not too major.'

But Helen was gazing into the distance. 'I wonder who we could ask to play Prince Charming.' She tapped her teeth with her pen. 'No one too old, nor anyone whose voice has barely broken. Hmm . . . I was wondering about one of those young men who work at the manor.'

'I'd suggest Wills and Kate from

down the road but Wills has come down with a lurgy.'

'But we have our new Cinders. How ill is he?'

Evie was about to protest when her mother yelled with delight. 'Why didn't it dawn on me before? Jake Vallance will make the perfect Prince Charming!'

9

Evie sat at the kitchen table, head in her hands, trying not to listen to her mother chatting up Jake on the landline. She'd rung the emporium, anxious to complete her casting, leaving her daughter secretly torn between delight and horror at the thought of setting herself up for total failure.

Helen returned with a triumphant look. 'Unlike you, he didn't take much persuading. Jake hasn't done any acting since his university days but said he'll give it a whirl. Isn't that wonderful?'

'Terrific. Not. Why can't you realise I'm a backroom girl, not a performer? Did you tell him I'd rather stick pins in my eyes than learn lines?'

'Don't be silly, dear. I told him you'd already agreed to take over as Cinderella and he seemed very pleased. Of course, like you, he doesn't have much of a social life, poor boy.'

Evie loved her mother but there were times when she could kill her. And this was one of them.

'Both Jake and I are out of our comfort zones, Mum. Our social lives are in London, remember?'

'Whatever you say, dear. Now, I've suggested you two meet so you can read through the script together. I've checked he has your mobile number and I've told him to ring and fix a date.'

'For goodness' sake, Mum!'

'Of course, this snow is very inconvenient but somehow we'll get by. Use Skype or something if we can't all manage to meet together in real life. Now, I must print off the scripts for our new Cinders and her Prince Charming. I doubt we'll ever see the original ones back! Honestly, some people . . . '

Please tell me I'm in the middle of a nightmare!

Deep down, Evie couldn't wait to hear Jake's voice again — but then she gasped as realisation struck. This was arguably the most popular pantomime ever, boy-meets-girl with bells on. And there would be no denying, once Cinderella's foot fit the slipper, the audience would expect Prince Charming to claim his bride with a kiss. She could feel herself blushing scarlet at the very thought.

★　★　★

Jake felt as though he'd been sledge-hammered, or mown down by a snowplough in the shape of the charming, community-minded Helen Meredith.

He was waiting for one of his most important customers to collect the jewellery the man had chosen for his wife's Christmas gift. Selling that magnificent ruby and diamond bracelet with matching ring would push up the shop's takings that week very satisfactorily.

Luckily for Vallance's Emporium, this client lived not far from the shop where sales had, of course petered out ever since the weather conditions turned Arctic. Their assistant, Susie, had gone down with some sort of lurgy but Jake was enjoying being alone. He'd already altered the window display — nothing too startling — but little touches added here and there.

That made him think of Evie and what she did for a living. Had she ever come into the shop, searching for something special needed for a television drama? Probably not. She must have London contacts and access to specialists.

She obviously planned on staying with her folks until after Christmas, now she'd committed herself to playing Cinderella. Her mother told him Evie had already agreed to take on the role, and that the script was an updated version of the traditional story. So how would she react to playing opposite him? How would she feel about an onstage kiss? Jake sat down in his father's beautiful old chair with its faded chintz seat and rested his head in his hands.

What madness had possessed him? Well, he knew the answer to that, didn't he? The moment he knew Evie was to be his leading lady, he'd behaved like a lovesick teenager! He should have refused, blaming having to run the business until his father was fit again. But now, if he rang Helen to say he'd made a wrong decision and couldn't possibly take on the part, Evie would assume he didn't want to share the stage with her and might understandably be very upset. What a nightmare!

No way would he risk hurting her. The memory of those solemn grey eyes, brimming with tears, looking up at him that first time they met, would stay with him for a very long time.

Yet, if he took the role, he could expect many awkward moments. How could he, Prince Charming, possibly gaze into Cinderella's eyes without revealing his true feelings? If he backed out, he'd lose a golden opportunity to get to know her better. And that was what he really longed for.

The doorbell catapulted him back to. the moment. He needed to put aside personal matters and concentrate on this important sale.

★   ★   ★

Evie opened up her laptop to check out the vicar's photographs. She called up the Mossford website and couldn't help smiling at the sight of the figures. Her hard work and her father's had paid off, with subtle lighting enhancing the effect. Mary's cerulean blue robe looked as natural as she'd hoped. Over on social media, she was surprised to see how many people were expressing approval, many sharing the photos so other folk were made aware of the beautiful Nativity scene. She hadn't thought of checking her accounts since being so busy with the tableau, then stopped in her tracks by the toxic Marcus.

Nor had she thought of blocking him so she didn't have to endure his comments. Here he was popping up, his words printed in white on a gaudy orange background, the equivalent of shouting to the world how he'd been so badly let down by his last girlfriend. Evie couldn't help feeling he'd got what he deserved.

But then her throat dried. How could she ever have thought Marcus might be the man for her? He was telling his friends that Chloe — a waif-like, blonde, fairly well-known model — had thrown over the exotic holiday he was planning to take her on, in favour of a modelling contract in Sydney.

The snake! Evie stared at the telltale comment. Had he no pride at all? But worst of all, he obviously must have thought Evie was so desperate for some winter sunshine that it was worth driving to the Cotswolds, hoping to persuade her to accompany him. It was small consolation to see that more than one of his so-called friends had posted comments saying it served him right for breaking off his relationship with Evie.

What rubbish it all was! But Evie felt tears stinging her eyelids and that annoyed her too, as she'd decided her fit of crying last weekend must be the last time she wept over any man.

Had Jake ever caused a girlfriend of his to burst into tears? Since he caught Evie so obviously in distress, that first chance meeting gave away much about his character. Even if she'd been curt in the way she spoke, he'd hopefully been aware that she hadn't been at her best. Since then, on the rare occasions when they relaxed and spoke freely, they got on well. Didn't this prove she was better to keep things on a friendly basis?

* * *

That evening, when her mobile rang, Evie felt a shiver of anticipation. Her parents were watching a film and she was in the kitchen with her beloved

Rusty. The red setter was curled in his basket, probably wondering what had happened to the long walks filled with lovely smells he usually enjoyed. His mistress was curled up in the comfy chair beside the Raeburn, lost in a book.

Rusty opened his eyes and looked at her with a mournful expression as she unwound herself and reached across to pick up her phone.

'Is this a bad time to call you?'

'Uh, no, it's fine.'

'To be honest, I'm wondering what we've let ourselves in for with this panto. But if you're up for it, I'll do my best not to let you down.'

'It's more likely to be the other way round.'

'Ha! You haven't seen me acting yet.'

She could hear the smile in his voice.

'It's not the lines I'm so worried about, actually. It's the songs.'

'What songs?'

She smothered a giggle. 'Cinders has a few tra-la-la lyrics but you and I have a duet when we meet in the forest and, um, fall in love.'

Silence. She waited, trying not to giggle.

'Are you still there, Jake?'

'Er, yeah. Yeah, sorry, Evie. I was just . . . contemplating. I think my singing might be marginally better than my acting.'

'Our duet's potentially a big show-stopper. Love at first sight.' She gulped. 'I'll probably need tranquillisers to get me through this.'

'No pressure, then.'

'No offence intended, but I think my mother might have done better to postpone the panto and put it on in February.'

'Any chance of that?' He sounded hopeful.

'Nope. I take it she didn't audition you either?'

'To be fair, she asked if I'd heard of *Cinderella*.'

Evie chuckled. 'You must've made a really good impression.'

'Your mother's a natural diplomat. She must be, if she can keep my father in order on that village hall committee. I gather you and I are supposed to meet for a read-through, but it's well below zero out there and conditions may be treacherous tomorrow. I'll head off to Elmchester in the morning but are you free in the evening if I can abseil down the slope to get to you?'

'I'll be here. According to my mother, I have no social life whatsoever.'

He groaned. 'I know the feeling. Mind you, I'm no party animal at the best of times.'

'This is the best conversation I've had all day.'

That gorgeous laugh rolled out of her phone. 'This is the only conversation I've had all day outside the shop. You're so easy to talk to, Evie.'

She blinked hard. 'Bet you didn't think that when I was so rude to you that first time.'

'You were upset. I butted in.'

'No, it was kind. I've moved on since then.'

'You sound very determined. Are you quite certain you don't want to be reconciled with him?'

'I'm one million percent sure!' Evie found herself telling Jake just how badly Marcus had treated her and how he followed it up by arriving in Lower Mossford with an invitation he must have figured she couldn't possibly refuse.

'My replacement, apparently a model called Chloe, didn't hang around long enough for him to try his tricks. She rejected his holiday of a lifetime offer in favour of a modelling job in Australia.'

Jake whistled. 'She did? And he imagined you'd take him back after the way he behaved? The guy must have some ego!'

'I can only think I must have been caught like a deer in headlights when he first paid me attention.' She hesitated. 'Enough! But thanks for listening. My friends in London were sympathetic, yet I couldn't help wondering if one or two were secretly pleased Marcus was available again.'

'And I thought the antiques trade was a rat race! I have a flat in London but I travel a lot. Hiding away in the Cotswolds like this is proving more enjoyable than I'd ever have thought. And I don't just mean because of the excellent ale they serve at The Wheatsheaf.'

Evie felt so hot, she decided she must have spent too much time beside the big stove. If Jake was flirting, it could surely only mean he was practising Prince Charming's wooing technique.

'Did Mum email you the script?' she asked.

'I've printed it and started marking Prince Wotsit's entrances and exits. He's quite a big cheese, isn't he?'

'Fortunately it's the Ugly Sisters, my evil stepmother and Buttons who have most to do. You and I don't need to try and raise a laugh.'

He answered so quietly, she was

about to ask him to repeat his remark, when she realised what he'd said.

'No, Evie. We just need to fall in love.'

10

Next day, Evie managed to take Rusty for a walk, despite the treacherous conditions underfoot. She kept to the grass verge, her boots crunching through the icy crust while Rusty found his paws in the white wonderland.

When she reached Kate's cottage, she sent a text saying she was outside if Kate needed any shopping. Moments later, the front door opened.

'Hooray! A human being to talk to, apart from Liam, of course!' Kate, wrapped in at least three jumpers, gave Evie a big smile. 'Wills is much better so he's gone back to work today and Liam's asleep. Do you fancy a coffee?'

'I'd better not, thanks. Rusty needs exercise. Mum says they've gritted the high street so I might try and stagger along to the church.'

'I'll be glad to get out again. We really

must try and visit the manor and I'm dying to see your Nativity scene. The photographs are great.'

'Aw, thanks, but my dad did the difficult stuff. The robes were simple to make, believe me.'

'Simple? For you, they were, perhaps!'

Evie had a sudden thought. 'Would you be interested in joining the cast of *Cinderella?* My mother's helping with casting and organising of rehearsals and stuff.'

'What exactly do you mean?'

'I've no idea how much acting you've done but it did occur to me that you and Wills would make the perfect Cinderella and Prince Charming.' Mentally, Evie was crossing her fingers.

Kate snorted. 'Thanks for the compliment, but while I might like the thought of playing the lead role, Wills would barricade himself in the bedroom at the thought of dressing up in tights!'

'Tights! I . . . I hadn't thought about

Prince Charming having to wear tights.'
Liar!

'Maybe it'll be a modern version, like they do with Shakespeare's plays sometimes.'

Temporarily lost for words, Evie nodded.

'Though I can't imagine Prince Charming in jeans and Cinders wearing a pair of funky leggings.' Kate looked thoughtful. 'Maybe next year, I can help with something. I used to be in the school choir, if that's any use.'

'I'm sure you'd be welcomed with open arms, but I thought I'd check whether you were longing to tread the boards, with or without Wills.'

'That's kind of you, Evie. I was wondering who'd take over the parts now. I wanted to email you and find out but I thought your mum might still be looking for replacements.'

'So you know about the big bust-up?'

'Yes.' Kate sighed. 'Poor girl. I don't know her well but we've spoken once or twice when we've met in the shop. What a rotten thing for her fiancé to do. I'm so lucky with Wills.' She nudged Evie. 'Hellooo? You suddenly looked far away. I hope I didn't bring back unhappy memories for you?'

'No, it's all right, Kate. I'd better get on. Sure there's nothing you want?'

'Loads of things,' Kate said cheerfully. 'But Wills was going to leave a list at the shop and he'll collect everything later. Take care, Evie.'

She gave Kate a quick hug. 'I promise to take you up on your offer of a cuppa before too long, and when the weather's better, we can take Liam to the manor. I'd really enjoy that.'

But as Evie set off again, she realised she'd learned something else about herself. Although she'd practically handed the role of Cinderella to her friend on a plate, the moment the words left her mouth, she'd felt a huge pang. It had been a heart-wrenching moment and all because, even though Kate was married to lovely Wills, the thought of her friend acting out a love scene with Jake wracked her with jealousy the likes of which she'd never experienced before.

★   ★   ★

One of the good things about living in Mossford was its community shop. Villagers donated unwanted books and CDs for other people to borrow and return, or to purchase. Although she streamed and downloaded stuff to watch, Evie found that section of charity shops irresistible.

She made sure Rusty's lead was secured before entering the shop where the elegant woman behind the till greeted her.

'Thank you for braving the elements. Can I help or do you know where to find what you want?'

'I might buy some chocolate but I'll just have a look at the books and CDs while it's quiet.'

'Someone brought in a pile just before that snow arrived and stopped us all in our tracks, so you may find some gems.'

'Too much to hope there'll be something to help with my non-existent acting skills!' Evie smiled at the woman who had beautifully-styled dark hair and lovely skin.

'Depends what you're after, I suppose.'

'I'm probably not going to find the latest *Cinderella* DVD?'

'Does that mean you're involved in the panto?'

'No choice. My mother's doing the casting.'

The woman smiled. 'You're Helen's daughter?'

'I'm Evie, yes. I'm between jobs just now so I've been helping update the Christmas tableau in the church — and now somehow I've joined the pantomime cast.'

'My son's been given a part too. I can't believe he agreed! It's totally out of character.'

To her annoyance, Evie's stomach

performed one of its spectacular lurches. She hoped she looked outwardly calm and politely interested.

'Which role is he playing?'

'He told me he was playing Prince Wotsit so I presume he means Prince Charming.'

With the benefit of this information, Evie could see the resemblance between Jake and his mum.

'I'm Annie. Good to meet you, Evie. Your mother mentioned you were home for a while, as Jake is of course. And now you'll be rehearsing together.'

'I wish I felt more confident but it helps to know he and I are in the same boat.'

Evie realised Annie was sizing her up. Did she know something? Had Jake said anything to make his mother suspect there might, just might, be the tiniest spark of attraction between her son and Helen Meredith's daughter?

'Of course, if you get to know each other and feel relaxed in each other's company, that alone will be a huge help.

And don't forget, the audience needs to sense the chemistry between two people who fall in love, like the fairy tale says.'

Evie stared at Jake's mum, taken aback. To her relief Annie Vallance remembered her duties.

'I need to begin a stock check so I'll leave you to it, my dear. Give me a yell if you need anything.'

Anne set off to the storeroom. She seemed very pleasant but Evie found some of her comments disturbing, almost as though she was sounding Evie out. Perhaps with a son as attractive as Jake, she couldn't help but feel protective.

Well, Evie wasn't about to make a play in his direction. Romance had lost its allure for her, thanks to Marcus. But she suspected she'd need all her determination to keep a distance between her and Jake, delightful as he might be. It would be difficult . . . but she could and would do it.

★   ★   ★

163

Driving home late afternoon, Jake almost missed his turning. Fortunately there wasn't much traffic but he heaved a sigh of relief at being only minutes away from Upper Mossford. What he needed now was a thaw. Once the pavements and roads were clear and safe again, the shop could return to its usual trading pattern. His father would cease to be terrified to step outside the house — not that Jake blamed him for that — and people would once more be able to walk up and down the slopes joining the two levels without feeling as though they might need a mountain rescue service.

Not that he resented having to walk down to the Merediths' house. Far from it. He liked Evie and they seemed to hit it off. OK, so maybe he liked her just a little too much. He hardly knew her and though she must never, ever, find out, the only reason he'd agreed to take part in the panto was that it meant seeing more of her. Except that the thought of kissing her with people looking on was beginning to worry him, even though that surely wouldn't happen yet. But it would become the elephant in the room, unless the pair of them relaxed and remembered this was all about a fairy tale. Not about real life.

He wondered how she felt about kissing him. That precious moment in the church when he forgot everything except the desire to feel her lips on his seemed a lifetime away., He'd said stuff he shouldn't have. Must have misread her expression. But making believe you'd fallen in love with the person you were kissing in the fictional world of Cinderella must be different from kissing the person you truly had fallen in love with.

If he really wanted her in his life, not just as a friend while they were both in limbo, so to speak, somehow he'd need to soften her resolve. And he felt pretty sure Evie was still smarting from the treatment she'd received from her ex-boyfriend.

Jake drove on to his drive, noting how his wheels squidged over snow still lying on the ground. Did that mean the temperature was rising slowly?

He got out and locked the car.

'Hi there!'

Jake turned his head to see a man standing inside the gateway. He was wearing a slightly too large overcoat that looked as though it belonged to someone else and he had a long black scarf wound around his neck several times. The green wellies on his feet added a bizarre touch.

'Can I help you?' Jake didn't move from the spot. The guy looked harmless enough, but life in London had taught him to be on his guard when faced with a situation he was unsure about.

'Sorry to intrude but I'm wondering how the roads are. Have you driven far to get here? I'm desperate to return to town.'

Jake walked towards him. 'I think we might be in for a thaw but I haven't checked the forecast. What kind of car do you have?'

'One without four-wheel drive. In fact, I've not moved it since I arrived the afternoon the snow began. What a waste of time this has been!'

Something in Jake's brain began nagging him, but first things first. He stepped cautiously from the snowy patch and on to the pathway he'd dug out and gritted. In his turn, the visitor moved a few steps forward.

'I wouldn't attempt to set off this evening, that's for sure,' Jake said. 'Hopefully you'll be good to go in the morning. If I were you, I wouldn't leave until around eleven when things should have warmed up a little.'

The other man nodded. 'Let's hope you're right. I came to this village to sort something out with my girlfriend, but she's let me down badly. Women, eh? Fortunately I've been able to stay with an old friend but I've had enough of her company now. What an airhead!'

Jake's uncertainty was solidifying into

something verging on anger. If this stranger was looking for sympathy, he'd chosen the wrong person. He'd no intention of asking, but he knew this man had to be Evie's ex.

'You may know Melissa McDonnell Brown? I guess so, as she's your local celebrity. Hey, don't tell her what I said, will you, mate?'

Jake scowled. Melissa was a client of his, not a close friend, but this fellow had been accepting her hospitality for days and here he was, running her down, as if he was acting in one of the soap operas she'd starred in.

'As for my girlfriend — ex-girlfriend, I should say — she's a right little you know what! Would you believe she refuses to come on holiday with me?' He made a sweeping gesture with both hands. 'I offer her Christmas in the Caribbean and the stupid little minx turns me down!'

Jake lunged at the other man and shoved his shoulder. As if in slow motion Marcus lost his balance and tumbled into the heaped-up, slightly grubby snow at the side of the drive.

'That's for Evie!' Jake yelled.

He wasn't an aggressive man but something in him snapped when he heard Evie being sneered about. He waited to make sure his unwelcome visitor was back on his feet before walking towards the house.

On his way, he called over his shoulder.

'And if I get to hear you've been in the pub tonight, bad-mouthing Evie again, you scumbag, just remember I have Melissa's phone number. Fancy a night in your car, do you?'

11

Much to Evie's relief, her mother and father were invited for a meal with friends living close by. Evie led Jake to the kitchen when he arrived for the script reading. They sat opposite one another at the table, their scripts ready at the point where Cinders met the handsome prince while walking in the forest.

'I have a confession to make.' Jake made a wry face.

'Please don't tell me you've changed your mind about taking the part.'

'No, of course not. I wouldn't do that to you — not when I know you're as apprehensive about it as I am. We're in this together. My confession is that my mother found a DVD of Disney's new version. She said you were in the shop today, looking through the second-hand ones there and that made her think of

Lisa's collection.'

'Sorry, but who's Lisa?'

'Ah, I should have said. Lisa's my kid sister. She's away on a gap year so she and her mates are enjoying the Australian sunshine.'

'Lucky Lisa.'

Jake wondered if Evie was regretting turning down her ex's invitation to travel to the Caribbean but resisted the impulse to say something. Instead, he pulled a DVD from the plastic folder he'd brought his script in and pushed it across the table.

'Maybe you've already seen this? My mother said I should watch it, but I doubt it'll help me.'

Evie looked at the cover picture. 'I haven't seen it. I like the actress playing Cinders but I don't know the guy in the prince's role. I wonder if we should watch this together.'

He shrugged. 'If you think we should, I'll try and survive.'

'It might be a good way to bond.' The moment the words left her lips, Evie regretted them. What if he took her comment as an invitation to get cosy? She felt she could die of embarrassment but the damage was done.

Jake's lips were quivering.

'What?' Evie couldn't help giggling. 'By the way, your face is a picture.'

'It seems such a girly thing to do.'

'Jake Vallance! Do you want to make a good job of this or not?'

'OK. I promise I'll take it seriously.'

Evie stood up. 'We'll be more comfortable in the sitting room. My laptop can sit on the coffee table and we can, um, sit on the settee.' She hesitated. 'Dad opened a bottle of wine for us. It's on the worktop. Would you like to pour two glasses while I sort things out?'

'Sounds good.' He rose. 'I See it. Glasses?'

'In the cupboard above the kettle.'

She was on her way to the sitting room when she realised she'd left the DVD in the kitchen. Cursing herself, she went back and tried to hide her mistake by improvising. 'Um, I should've asked, did you eat before you came down here?'

Their gazes locked. Her pulse was racing.

'I'm fine, thank you.' He inspected the wine label. 'Your father has good taste.'

Evie was convinced he had something on his mind beside her dad's knowledge of French wines, but their reason for meeting was to read through the panto script so they'd better get on with watching how the professionals did it.

Somehow they managed to arrange themselves on the settee without sitting too close together. It seemed to her Jake felt just as she did. In a way, it was a relief. In another way, it made her yearn for what she was missing.

She took a sip of wine and tried to concentrate. He teased her about keeping a notebook at the ready; she insisted she was being businesslike.

When Cinderella was galloping through

the woods and encountered that magnificent stag, Evie sat up straight, knowing the huntsman prince couldn't be far away.

'She's a feisty young woman,' Jake commented. 'Way to go, Cinders!'

'I wonder if our scriptwriter watched this film. Cinderella's being bullied by her horrendous new family but she's not afraid to give the prince a piece of her mind.'

'Ah, but does she realise she's telling off royalty and not just any old huntsman?'

'Shush. See that look he's giving her? Do you think you could manage to look at me like that?'

'With practice, yes, I'm sure I could. Not so sure about bringing horses and a stag into the village hall though . . .'

Evie was enjoying herself far too much. What had seemed a good idea might well prove a poisoned chalice. Whoops, wrong fairy tale!

'D'you want me to fast forward this bit?'

'Perhaps we should watch it all. Learn about the characters' motivation?'

'Whatever you think.'

When they reached the fairy godmother scene, Evie suggested Jake topped up their glasses. He came back as Cinders was arriving at the ball.

'Quick! Prince Charming's just spotted Ella.'

Jake handed her glass to her and slid back on to the settee. She caught a waft of aftershave even though his chin was shadowed with dark stubble. Evie swallowed hard. The chemistry between the two stars was fizzing. Would she and Jake succeed in acting even a fraction as well?

She made notes, biting back tears once or twice when Ella's wicked stepmama and her grim daughters behaved particularly badly. Beside her, Jake made an occasional comment but mostly kept his attention fixed on the screen until the movie ended and he excused himself.

She busied herself, removing the DVD and picking up their empty glasses. She'd reached the kitchen and heard Jake closing the cloakroom door again behind him when the room was suddenly plunged into darkness.

★　★　★

'Evie? Are you all right?'

'Yep. I'm sure there's a torch around here somewhere but I need to find the candles too.'

'I'm using my phone torch.'

'Good thinking. No idea where I left my mobile. I wonder if it's just us, or whether the whole of Lower Mossford is blacked out. I hope it isn't due to so many people having Christmas lights on.'

'It might be the trip switch. Any idea where . . . ?'

'Sorry, it's never occurred to me to find out.'

'That's OK. I'll shine this around. Maybe try the utility room first?'

'Whatever you think best.' Evie was opening and closing drawers. 'Maybe Mum keeps candles in there too. She's bought gold and silver ones for Christmas but I don't want to light those.'

'Let's hope we find some kitchen ones. And matches or a cigarette lighter?'

'We're all non-smokers. There must be matches if we can only find the candles. The range is all electric.'

'What about tapers? I could light one from the wood burner. We'll keep on looking. If you come in here with me, I'll shine my phone torch around.'

He was in the utility room. Cautiously, Evie moved towards the door from the kitchen. She could hear Jake talking to the dog. Rusty was probably enjoying the attention. She must remember to let him out soon.

Evie moved towards the tiny light beam.

'Yay!' On the shelf above the washing machine she'd spotted a big black flashlight.

'Excellent.' Jake moved closer.

She was achingly conscious of him beside her as he reached for the torch and placed it on the washing machine. She wasn't sure who made the first move, but all of a sudden his arms were around her and she was clasping her hands around his neck.

'Evie?'

'Sssh.'

Their lips met. She closed her eyes even though neither of them had switched on the torch yet and Jake had clicked off his phone light. He was kissing her as though he never wanted to let her go. She tasted wine on his lips. Or was it on hers? Gently his tongue teased hers and she could swear she could see falling stars. Or was it she who was falling? Falling . . . falling in love . . .

If she'd been concerned about chemistry sparking between her panto-mime character and his, there was absolutely no need. But this kiss must be forgotten. It was obviously sparked by those two delicious glasses of Beaujolais. Everyone knew how alcohol could dissolve people's inhibitions. And the sudden darkness must have caused her to become disorientated.

Suddenly he'd stopped kissing her. But he still held her tight. Still made her feel as though they were the only two people in the world.

'Darling Evie, is this all right? I want to kiss you again.'

She lifted her face to his. *I'm only behaving as Cinderella would in the same circumstances.*

Tomorrow, she and Jake would return to being friends and fellow actors. Any spark between them would be down to their acting, such as they were. But, tonight, she couldn't resist tasting the magic sizzling between them just one more time.

★　★　★

Jake had located the trip switch and the power was on again. Evie told him it served her right for not being more organised. He offered to take the dog out. She accepted. When he returned, she offered to make coffee. He refused.

'I don't know about you, but I'd prefer to leave the script reading till tomorrow.'

'That's fine by me,' she said. 'Watching the DVD was helpful, I think.'

'Definitely.' He was checking his watch.

'But it's still not late.'

He frowned. Pulled out a chair. She still stood beside the range. Last time she stood in this position, Marcus was lounging where Jake sat now. She tried to close her mind to all that.

'Evie, I need to tell you something.'

He's married. His wife's a scientist and she's away on an important assignment overseas. That's fine. Nothing's happening between us. What's a kiss or two between friends?

Jake was staring at his hands, clasped in front of him on the table. She wanted him to get to his feet, knocking the chair over in his haste to kiss her again. But that wasn't going to happen. Nor should it. She'd had her glass slipper moment. The sooner they acknowledged what happened between them mustn't happen again, the better for both of them.

'I've done something very wrong.'

Her body tensed.

'When I got home today, I talked to someone who was wanting to know what the roads were like. He said he'd been marooned in the village since he arrived the day the snow started.'

Evie's throat performed its familiar trick of seizing up in times of stress.

'I'm not going to relate the conversation and I can tell by your face you've guessed who it was.'

She nodded. 'My ex.'

'I didn't ask his name but I twigged it must be Marcus. He said he'd been staying with a friend.'

She nodded again. 'That would be Melissa.'

'Correct. Evie, I ended up shoving the guy over into the snow.' He raised both hands and shook his head. 'I loathe violence, but some of his comments were so unpleasant, I lost control — but believe me, I didn't punch his lights out.'

'What a shame.'

Jake's face was ashen beneath the fluorescent ceiling light. Candlelight would have been more appropriate for this confession . . .

'This is the thing. I have no idea whether Marcus will lodge a complaint with the police. It'll be his word against mine. Yes, he was on Vallance land, but I answered his question about road conditions and offered advice. When I lunged at him, he lost his balance and fell into the snow.'

Evie pictured the scene and bit her lip. She had an awful urge to laugh but Jake was clearly upset.

'And I . . . well, actually I threatened him.'

'With what?'

'It doesn't matter. The only thing in my favour is that he didn't only say things about his ex.'

'Is that supposed to be me?'

'Sorry?'

'It's just that Marcus dumped me for a model named Chloe. She turned down his holiday invitation, which is why he decided to drive to Mossford and persuade me to go with him. He needed a plus-one to show off to his friends.'

'So, he finished his relationship with you, then took up with this Chloe who rejected him, which serves him right, of course. But he also sneered at Melissa and that got up my nose, knowing she'd taken him in when he was stranded.'

Evie felt a pang of jealousy. Why, oh why, did her body have to react in such an irritating manner when Jake mentioned some other girl's name?

'She'd given him hospitality, for goodness' sake! So I threatened to ring her if he gave you any more trouble.'

'And what would you have said?'

183

He closed his eyes for a beat or two. Boy, those eyelashes! Then he opened them again. Such a dreamy sea-green shade.

'I'd have confessed to assaulting her house guest because of how he treated you and how he'd insulted her. I'd have told her how much you already mean to me. I'd have let her know how much I detest bullies, rudeness and ingratitude.'

Evie, stunned by his throwaway remark, about what she meant to him, saw a smile touch his lips for the first time since they kissed.

'I might have told Marcus I had her mobile number and how did he fancy sleeping the night in his car. Well, something along those lines.'

'Thanks for telling me. I'm so sorry you had to put up with my ex's appalling behaviour. You must wonder what on earth I saw in him.'

His face was expressionless. 'It's none of my business.' He got to his feet. 'Better be on my way. It's, um, well, been a great evening. I can't pretend not to wish our relationship could be different, but obviously you have issues, Evie, and I accept that.'

She watched him shrug into his jacket, afraid to speak for fear of bursting into tears. Maybe he sensed that because he gave her a quick hug, as a brother might, or an old university buddy who'd fallen in love with your roommate.

'Text me when you're ready to tackle that script,' he said as he left.

12

Next morning, sunshine was making icicles drip and snow melt. It would probably take a while before the landscape returned to normal but Evie's family, like many others, felt very relieved.

The phone rang as they were breakfasting.

'Shall I get it?'

Evie's mum, mouth full of cornflakes, nodded. Her father was reading the morning paper, delighted to have it delivered at its usual hour now Lower Mossford was more easily accessible.

Evie answered after the fifth ring and recognised the caller's voice.

'Hi, Vicar. Is everything all right?'

'If you mean our beautiful Nativity tableau, everything's very much all right, thank you.'

'That's good. So, did you want to speak to Mum or to my dad?'

'You'll do very well, my dear. I imagine you've noticed the interest St Stephen's has been receiving on social media?'

'Well, yes, a bit, but I've pretty much had my hands full — ' She closed her eyes, remembering those hands caressing the back of Jake's head and neck. *Stop it, Evie!*

'Well, no pun intended, but everything has snowballed and I've just received a telephone call from the local TV station.'

'Really? What are they after?'

'They want to come and film a live feature for their morning show. They're sending one of their reporters to interview everyone involved with creating the Christmas tableau. Isn't that great? Of course, with this publicity, I'm hoping we'll get more worshippers at our services.'

'Fantastic. I'm very pleased for you.'

'May I count on you and your father joining me at the church tomorrow morning for the filming?'

'Goodness, I suppose so, but what about the person who made the original figures?'

'I did enquire about that when I first moved here, but the gentleman's apparently no longer with us. So it's really just you and Charlie and I'll be there in my official capacity. It's a seven-thirty start, I'm afraid.'

Evie gulped. 'That really is early. But we'll be there. I'll go and break the news to Dad now.'

★　★　★

Jake was up earlier than usual the following morning, determined to get off to the emporium and work on his Christmas theme display window. He was in the kitchen microwaving a bowl of porridge while his mother, having made a pot of tea, was switching on their small TV.

He was reaching for the jar of honey when his mother exclaimed, 'Wow! Look, there's Charlie Meredith with the vicar. I didn't realise the Nativity scene was creating such interest.'

Jake looked up at the screen and dropped his spoon. Evie's dad was talking about his renovation work on the wooden figures. The vicar, beaming, was nodding his head.

Then Jake saw Evie's face smiling back at him. He forgot all about porridge and honey as he gazed into her lovely eyes. His mother stopped talking and they focused on the screen.

'So, Evie, I gather you work in London but you're at home before beginning a new contract?'

Jake could tell by her body language that she was uncomfortable having her personal life explored on television.

'Well, yes, I'm between jobs. That's how I came to be roped in to help. Which I was very happy to do, of course,' she added hastily.

'Which is your favourite figure, Evie?'

The camera panned slowly across the tableau.

'I'm particularly pleased with Mary.'

'She has a very sweet face,' the presenter chimed in.

'Thank you. I'm still not sure I did too well with the eyes of one of the wise men.'

'Well, maybe we can be the judges of that. Let's have a close-up of your handiwork, please.'

A slow smile spread across Jake's face as he watched. He hadn't known her long, but this was so typical. She was sparking up an otherwise bread and butter interview. Now, viewers all over the area would be curious to see what she meant.

'Aha!' The presenter had twigged. 'The king bearing the gold — he has a very roguish look.' The presenter spoke straight to camera. 'What do you think, ladies and gentlemen? Is it something in his eyes? Does he remind you of someone, maybe? We'd love to have your comments via our usual social media . . . ' He went on to explain contact details. Then he turned back to Evie.

'Any more projects lined up, Evie?'

Evie stared at him, a horrified look on her face.

'I'm, helping with the panto. That's it, really.'

'Aha!' The vicar wasn't having that. 'Evie's kindly offered to take on the important role of Cinderella herself — and at very short notice.'

'Well done!' The presenter pushed his microphone towards her again. 'Do you have to make your own ball gown?'

'Fortunately, our vicar's wife and a couple of the WI ladies are making the costumes. I'm happy to do any alterations mine might need.'

The vicar nodded. 'We have such a wonderful community spirit in Mossford. Both Upper and Lower, of course.' He indicated Jake's churn. 'That addition to the scene has been kindly donated by the owners of an antiques emporium in Elmchester. And volunteers have been making sure as many fairy lights as possible will brighten the wintry gloom during this holy festive season.'

The presenter was obviously running out of time and quickly turned to Evie again.

'And what about your Prince Charming?'

Jake froze. His mother shot him a glance and tittered. Jake was watching Evie's face.

'Um. I don't think he gets to wear a ball gown.'

The presenter roared with laughter. Even the vicar chuckled. Evie and her father exchanged glances.

'Touché! Well, let's hope the lucky man looks good in his tights and thigh boots. Is Prince Charming played by the traditional principal boy?'

Evie seemed to look straight at Jake. 'He's very much a grown man, I'm glad to say.'

'Well, break a leg, Evie, you and all your cast.'

'Th . . . thanks. I think!'

The presenter faced the camera. 'Isn't she a star? We'll be back later when we have a trio of choirboys singing us a carol before school — '

Jake's mother turned down the sound. Jake picked up his spoon to eat his porridge.

'Well, that was fun,' said Mrs Vallance. 'I keep meaning to ask you, Jake. That comment about tights . . . what *will* Prince Charming be wearing?'

★   ★   ★

The vicar's wife came to the door quickly when Evie rang the bell later that morning.

'Aha, the star of the panto! Do come in.' She held the door open. 'I must tell you how relieved I was that you and your father could help out with those figures. This is such a hectic time of year.'

'Thanks, Louise, but I've decided the limelight isn't the place for me. I'm still trembling after that interview. The vicar came over well, Mum said.'

'Being a clergyman, Paul's always talking to people, isn't he? Of course, he's on a high because of the interest in the Nativity scene.'

'I never dreamed how much buzz there'd be. It's good for the church, though.'

'I think so, too. The primary school children are coming to see it, class by class, over the next couple of days. But I imagine you're here to see your Cinders costumes? I've got everything on a rail in the sitting room.'

Evie followed her. Whether she liked it or not, she daren't change her mind about taking part in the show, even though the thought was terrifying.

'Now we're losing all that snow, people are calling in to try their costumes. I hope we won't need to do much alteration for you. You're very similar in build to your predecessor. Do you have time to try these on or will you take them home?'

'I'll take them with me, thanks. I never thought I'd get so involved with village life.'

Louise shot her an appraising look. 'Sometimes things happen for a reason. They stop us in our tracks, make us consider other options.'

'I expect my mother's told you about my broken relationship.'

'She did. I hope you're not too devastated.'

'I was at first, but I've come to realise it was a good thing to be free of him. He's a very controlling person and he totally dazzled me for the first few months. He's quite well-known in his line of business and I think I was flattered that he singled me out and asked for a date.'

'That's understandable. Your mum said he turned up out of the blue to see you?'

'That's right. He was pretty unpleasant but Dad saw him off.' She gave a little huff as she thought of Jake's confession. 'Do you think it's wicked to push someone over?'

'I can't imagine Charlie Meredith doing so, but it sounds as though he was only being protective.'

'It, um, it wasn't Dad who shoved Marcus. It was Jake Vallance. I'm worried my ex-boyfriend might complain to the police, but it sounds as though Jake frightened him off.'

'Jake Vallance, hmm?' Louise's eyes sparkled. 'Sounds like he's taking his Prince Charming duties seriously!'

'Oh, no, no . . . there's nothing between us in real life. He came across Marcus by chance and couldn't stomach what he was saying. He's a loyal friend, even if I haven't known him long.'

'That's good to hear. Is your ex-boyfriend still in the village?'

'I hope he's left by now. He was marooned by the snow and was put up by a friend.'

Louise nodded. 'I heard something about Melissa McDonnell-Brown and some young man, but I try to ignore that sort of gossip.'

'He was anxious to return to London so when he spotted Jake in the driveway, he began talking to him and throwing his weight around, from what I gather. I really hope Jake doesn't suffer through this. I think my father would make a good character witness if it came to a police investigation.'

'Let's hope there aren't any repercussions.' Louise picked a hanger off the rail. 'How about this for a ball gown?'

Evie chuckled. 'That's great! Limp grey fabric, a couple of patches and a handkerchief hem.'

Louise held up the ball gown next, letting it sway gently on its hanger. 'Pretty, isn't it? That shade of blue suited our first Ella and it certainly does good things for you. This dress was our elder daughter's prom gown in its first incarnation.'

'Wow, I'm honoured.'

'I'm delighted you're taking on the role. Now, if you're talking to Jake, could you remind him he needs to try on his Prince Charming kit, please?'

'Yes, but I'm not sure when we're meeting up next.' *Remember what*

happened at the first attempt, Evie?
'Dare I ask what he has to wear?'

'I'm sure Jake won't mind you seeing it first.' Louise picked out a huntsman's brown tunic and trousers. 'I'm hoping he has suitable boots, otherwise we'll need to ask around.' She replaced the hanger and moved to the far end of the rail. 'Here's his highness's party suit.' Now she held up a dark green jacket and trousers. 'This will tone well with your blue-green frock.'

Evie had a feeling the trousers might be too short for Jake's long legs.

'I'm sure he'll be relieved he doesn't have to wear tights,' she said with a smile.

★　★　★

Evie's phone buzzed on her way home. Louise had placed her outfits in a plastic carrying bag. Now she was hanging on to it while she delved in her pocket, eager to see who'd texted her.

But it wasn't Jake. Kate was asking

whether Evie would like to walk to the manor that afternoon?

Kate was the only female friend her age she'd made in the village. A shame that she would have to put her off. Some of her London mates were girlfriends of Marcus's cronies and she had no doubt whose side they'd take, if forced to choose.

She decided to call at the shop and park her dress bag. One of her mum's friends was on duty, so she took Evie's burden while she phoned Kate.

Evie was halfway down the slope when her mobile buzzed again. It might be her phone provider. It might be Jake. Before she left London, she'd sent off her CV for the job based in Switzerland, not with any great hopes, but in an effort to motivate herself rather than sink into too deep a pit of gloom.

She decided not to risk the dress bag slipping from her grasp while she juggled thumbs and phone. There were still piles of snow around, though it now looked dingy and tired. Evie slotted her key in the front door lock and once inside, parked her costumes in the sitting room.

On checking her phone, she sucked in her breath. 'I don't believe it!'

Evie, we'd like you to attend an interview. Please confirm so we can email details.

★   ★   ★

Jake concentrated on his window display while Susie, now back to full health, sorted through a box of antique greetings cards. She'd already told him there were some beautiful Christmas cards among the collection and she was sorting everything into different categories.

Trade wasn't brisk but they'd sold a Victorian footstool and a beautiful 1950s doll. His mother would have loved to keep this but there was no excuse for holding on to items when, after the festive season, the business faced its two bleakest trading months.

Although their accountant was pleased with the business' progress, Jake was anxious to maintain a steady cash flow.

This didn't stop his mind from wandering. He and Evie needed to knuckle down and stick to the script. She was gorgeous, but he knew she was still hurting and, despite those stolen kisses, Jake didn't see how he could ever melt her heart.

He edged past the fir tree Susie had decorated in Victorian style. They didn't dare light real candles but they'd acquired a set of look-alikes. Now he needed a cup of coffee and a quick email check. Oh, yes, and he would text Evie. Would this evening be too short notice?

It was a pity they couldn't meet in the village hall, but it would be freezing in there. You couldn't expect the heating to be switched on just for the two of them. Soon they'd be rehearsing with the rest of the cast, so he wanted to get his act together. Jake called up Evie's name and typed out his message.

Are you free for a script reading tonight? You could come to mine. Will drive you home afterwards. Failing that, I'm free tomorrow night.

He was free for every foreseeable night between now and Christmas, but that seemed too sad a confession to make. But hadn't they each confided their lack of social life while back in the country?

Jake pressed Send.

13

Evie made for the utility room where Rusty gave her a warm welcome. She opened the door to the back garden and the dog bounded out. It was safely enclosed and she could leave him a few minutes while she made a coffee.

She needed to think, and to think quickly. When she'd prepared her drink, she went through and called Rusty back inside.

'We'll go for a lovely walk soon, boy, I promise.' Evie wiped off his paws one by one and the dog pattered off and settled into his basket with a chewy treat to occupy him.

She sat down to consider her options. Having applied for a job she felt was out of her league, she felt stunned to be invited to an interview. They must have liked something about her qualifications and experience.

If they offered her the contract, they probably wouldn't need her to start until the New Year.

Evie was staring into space when her phone buzzed again. Straight away she picked it up and read Jake's message. He wanted a script reading tonight? Normally she'd have said that was fine, but now she wasn't so sure.

Evie, don't hide from him. He's the man who rescues you from your horrible stepmother's clutches in the Mossford Christmas pantomime, for goodness' sake!

She'd committed herself to this production and she owed it to everyone to try her best. Not pulling her weight would cause a lot of hassle to people she cared about, including her mum. For a moment she contemplated persuading Kate to take over the role, but again, this made her feel devastated as she imagined herself breaking the news to Jake.

She answered his message, confirming she could come to his house at seven, but not mentioning his offer of a lift home. Next, she replied to the interview offer and confirmed her acceptance. Hopefully they wouldn't want to see her tomorrow, but if that happened, she knew Kate would understand.

Her mother's comment about her lack of social life was coming back to haunt her! Even if she wasn't caught up in a whirl of pre-Christmas parties, at this rate she seemed unlikely to have much free time to herself.

★　★　★

Evie's father walked her to the Vallances' driveway, insisting, as he'd been indoors all day, that he needed the fresh air.

Jake's mother let her in.

'Jake's on the phone to a client but let me take your coat. He won't be long. I lit a fire in the dining room, so you can do your read-through in there.'

'Thanks, Annie. How are your

Christmas preparations going?'

'The puddings and the cake are safely stowed away and thanks to the snow, I've written all my cards, and sent off the overseas ones now. It's unusual for me to have got that far by this stage of December.'

'I'm impressed. It hadn't occurred to me to ask Mum if she wants anything done.'

'I'm not surprised. No sooner were you home than you were grabbed to do all that work on the Nativity figures. The whole thing does you credit, Evie. No wonder the television people did a feature.'

'Thanks, but as I keep saying, Dad did the important stuff.'

'Definitely a team effort, I'd say.' Annie led the way to the dining room where a log fire glowed.

'Ooh, lovely. It's good to see a real fire.' Evie put her script down on the table where she noticed Jake's folder already at the other end.

'I'll bring a pot of tea through in

about an hour. Does that sound OK?'

'It certainly does.' Evie knew she was unlikely to get carried away by drinking a nice cup of tea.

'Any more publicity things coming your way?'

'The local paper's been in touch with the vicar so I expect I'll have to talk to a reporter, unless I talk Dad into doing it. They're going to take photos of the children when they visit the church, so people will love that.'

Evie turned as Jake appeared.

'I'm sorry to keep you waiting.'

'I'm a bit early. Dad fancied some fresh air so we walked here at a cracking pace.'

'Shall we begin?' He pulled out a chair for Evie.

He sounds so brisk and businesslike. But isn't that for the best?

She sat down. 'So it's the forest scene, yes?'

'Yep, where you're walking along the path, telling the audience how sad you feel.'

'And I hear the sound of the hunt in the distance . . . '

'And I suddenly appear because I've fallen off my horse and . . . ' He paused. 'Not a very dignified thing to happen to Prince Charming, is it?'

She chuckled. 'Especially when the maiden you find picking wild herbs tells you off for trying to stalk and kill wild and beautiful animals.'

'Quite right too. In your own time, then, Evie.'

She made a face at him and began her speech. *'But who is this I see, striding through the forest? He must be one of the hunting party from the castle.'* She looked up. 'I put my basket down now and stand there, hands on hips, waiting to reprimand you.' She pouted.

Jake cleared his throat. 'Um, that's good. I bow and smile at you. *Excuse me, miss, but I'm searching for my horse.'* He broke off. 'You're not supposed to laugh!'

She clapped her hand to her mouth.

'I wonder if we could alter the script there? Maybe you could say your horse bolted?'

'That sounds better. I'll make a note to suggest it, but maybe keep going for now.'

They were still reading when Jake's mother arrived with a tea tray. Jake poured two cups.

'Do you want a break or shall we continue?'

She didn't immediately answer.

'Evie, I know this must be difficult for . . . '

'Let's keep going, shall we?'

He nodded. 'I'm suspicious your stepmother has something to hide so I order my guards to search the house.' He looked at her. *'Ella's father must have been a prize idiot, marrying that evil woman!'*

'I don't think we should alter the script so drastically. We really would lose the plot then.'

To her surprise, as they continued, Evie felt genuinely sad and frightened that she wouldn't be found and Prince Charming would go away, shattering her one chance of happiness now her father had been killed and wouldn't be coming home to save her from her wretched existence. Lovely Ella was a slave, poor girl!

They completed the reading and sat back in their chairs, trying not to look at one another.

'That wasn't as bad as I imagined it'd be.'

'How much do you know by heart?' Evie felt curious.

'I'm learning some lines each night now, hoping they'll sink in while I sleep. How about you?'

'Same as you. It's been a hectic few days.' She looked at the logs glowing in the fireplace. 'I've been invited to an interview for a position I thought I had no chance of being considered for.'

'That's brilliant news. In London?'

'Yes, but I'm waiting for more information. Hopefully, if they can see me around noon, I can drive up and down in one day.'

'And still be back in time for rehearsal.'

'Well, yes, it's only going to be the one interview, I hope.'

He folded his arms behind his head. 'If you're successful, will you be based in London?'

'As far as I know. I might need to look for alternative accommodation. At the moment it suits me well to have my share of the rent paid by Ben's girlfriend — he's my flatmate — but I'm not sure I want to play gooseberry.'

'Understandable. I have friends staying at my place. They're between houses and when my father started having health problems, I decided to move down here for a few weeks. It's certainly no hardship.' He was staring at the flames.

'Have you tried on your costumes yet?'

He grimaced. 'Yes, but the huntsman's and the prince's posh trousers are on the short side. I'm hoping I can tuck them into my boots.'

'If you come to our house next time, bring both outfits and I'll see if I can let the hems down.'

'That'd be very kind. My mother's a fantastic cook and not bad at knitting but when I was at school, I learned quickly how to sew on a button.'

'Good for you.' Evie stood up. 'Could we wait until they send my interview time before we agree on our next date . . . um, I mean our next rehearsal?'

She noticed the little creases around his eyes as he smiled. 'Apart from tomorrow night when I'm driving my father to a dinner he thinks he's fit enough to attend, my social calendar's pretty much empty. But you know that, don't you?'

*   *   *

Jake drove Evie home. The night was clear and frosty, stars glittering like crystals on black velvet.

'It's beautiful, isn't it? Where would

you prefer to be, Evie? Back in London with all that hustle, or here in the sticks?' Jake had started the engine and was letting the windscreen clear.

'One thing I've decided is, if I get this job in London, I'll make sure I come home to Mossford more often than I did before.'

'I know what you mean. We're lucky to have our roots in a village like this one.'

She didn't confide how Marcus had monopolised her attention over the last months, and how he'd only conde-scended to meet her folks once when they were visiting London, but she had the feeling Jake understood. Sometimes she detected sadness in his eyes hinting at some tragic event buried in his memory, possibly surfacing when he was faced with a reminder. He knew more about her romantic back-story than she did about his, but no way did she intend prying.

Jake drove the short distance down to her folks' cottage. He deliberately went slowly so they could look at the various displays of Christmas lights along the way. Evie couldn't help sounding like an excited child as she exclaimed over the more elaborate ones.

'I think the village has done an excellent job this year.' He drew up outside her gate. 'Your mother certainly galvanised everyone into action.'

'Scared them witless, more like!'

Jake laughed. She turned to face him, feeling her pulse race as he reached out to touch her mouth with his forefinger. 'Goodnight, Cinderella. I fear I must leave you now before my trusty estate car turns into a pumpkin.'

She waited to see if he would follow up with a goodnight kiss, but he sat staring straight ahead. This was her cue to go indoors. Surely keeping their relationship to one of friendship only was what she'd decided she wanted?

'Goodnight, Prince. I'll be in touch. Don't forget to bring your costumes when we meet next time.'

'I'll look forward to it. I hope the

interview goes well and, meanwhile, I promise not to hunt any magnificent wild beasts. Take care.'

She watched the two red dots of his tail lights disappear into the gloom. As she let herself into the house, she could hear the television in the sitting room, so popped her head round the door.

'How did the rehearsal go, darling?'

'Not too badly, thanks. We think we need to do one more reading just with the two of us so I've suggested Jake comes here again next time.'

'That's fine, darling. Night-night then.'

Evie left them to their film, smiling as she realised tonight's choice had actually been released in the twenty-first century. In her room, she opened up her laptop and checked her emails. So far there was nothing regarding her interview. But as a new message arrived, she realised it was from Marcus.

Evie opened it with a feeling of foreboding. She didn't put it past him to have talked to people about her job-hunting plans and warn them off, but surely he wouldn't really take such spiteful action? And now he was safely back in London and no longer in need of Melissa's hospitality, Jake's stern warning no longer held its original power. Although sorely tempted to delete the email, she began reading.

Evie, I have given much thought to what happened between your friend and me, the afternoon before I drove back to London. Because of the close relationship that once existed between us, I'm prepared not to lodge a formal complaint of assault by the man Melissa informed me is called Jake Vallance. On one condition . . .

She pursed her lips as she scanned the text. *If you come to London and join me on Saturday's flight to our holiday destination, I will give you my signed agreement not to pursue matters regarding Mr Vallance. In addition, I shall require you to be at my side throughout the Christmas festivities on*

216

the island. You'll need to arrive in London in plenty of time for me to take you shopping for any clothes you may need before we leave for the airport.

I think you'll agree that under the circumstances, my offer is most generous. I hope you'll also decide to let bygones be bygones, especially when I tell you that I may well be able to help you obtain your next contract.

You surely cannot wish to bury yourself in that claustrophobic village any longer than necessary.

Call me when you receive this message, Evie. I don't have time for arguments.

Marcus

14

Jake was propped against his pillows, reading his script when he heard an email arrive. His curiosity was stirred when he saw who sent it.

If these were script change suggestions, then she must be very keen. He'd need to up his game in order to keep pace.

Hi. Sorry to trouble you, but I've received a very disturbing message from my ex and having given it much thought, I'm forwarding it to you.

I can only apologise for Marcus's behaviour and obviously I wish you hadn't been involved. My first reaction was to do what he sets out in his letter, and travel to London tomorrow.

But then I started to consider the other side of things. Why should I agree to spend two weeks with a man I've come to hate and distrust, keeping up the pretence of being his girlfriend? OK, maybe I could handle that, horrible though it would be, knowing at the end of it, I'd have his agreement not to press charges against you.

But then I thought of the hassle I'd be causing so many people. Cinderella isn't just any old village panto. Since I've been home, I've come to realise how much work goes into such a production. If I pulled out, my mother would have to find a replacement and I know, even though I probably wind them up at times, my folks love having me around.

To be honest, Jake, I'm feeling mixed up and would appreciate your opinion. You may not read this tonight but when you do, could you please let me have your thoughts?

Your friend, Evie

*   *   *

Jake read her message through twice then sighed in exasperation. What a low-life Marcus was! How dare he use such bully-boy tactics? No way should Evie be expected to cancel her own plans and jump to his selfish demands.

Jake typed out his response and sent it.

★   ★   ★

Evie had cried herself to sleep. Next morning, she dragged herself out of bed and went through her morning rituals before going downstairs.

'All right, darling?' Her father was in his usual chair, drinking tea, and doing a crossword. His world must be the same as it was yesterday. To his daughter, nothing felt right.

'Not too bad, thanks, Dad.'

Her mother was making toast. 'You look pale, Evie. Can you manage a couple of slices?'

Despite her gloom, it seemed a long time since she'd eaten. 'Yes, please. I'll grab a tangerine too, if I may.'

'Burning the candle at both ends?'

Her father looked up from his puzzle. 'You used to be speedy when it came to learning by heart in your schooldays.'

'I'm fine. Don't fuss, Dad.'

Charlie raised his eyebrows.

Evie noticed her mother glance over her shoulder. She didn't want her current anxiety to cause an upset with her parents. Diversion tactics were needed.

'Sorry. I'm just a bit edgy because I heard yesterday I'm being considered for a job. I emailed back to say I could attend for interview but I'm waiting to see what they say. I do need a new contract, you know that.'

'Yes, of course, and that's good news, darling. But I hope it doesn't mean you'll be rushing back to London and starting work immediately?'

Whoops! Mum didn't take long to work that out.

'My interview will be in London, but I doubt very much I'll get the job. And if I did, it's probably too close to Christmas to expect me to start work.'

'Phew!' Helen smiled her relief. 'Apart from having you around of course, I'd need to cast my net to find another Cinders. Jake would be disappointed too.'

'Let's not be pessimistic. Hopefully I'll hear back today and I can plan ahead then.'

Must my mother smile so knowingly?

★ ★ ★

Evie's mobile rang while she was trying to convince herself it was worth adjusting the neckline of her pantomime ball gown while still uncertain whether she'd still be playing the part.

'Hi Jake, I'm so sorry to have bothered you.'

'You were absolutely right to do so. What are you up to this morning?'

'Besides learning lines? I'm not even sure it's worth doing that at the moment.'

She heard him suck in his breath. 'I can imagine. So, we need to get our act together. I have to be at the shop, as our assistant isn't coming in until two. I, um, wondered whether you fancied a day away from it all. Come to Elmchester with me and we can talk properly, one to one, and find a solution to this problem.'

Evie swallowed hard. 'That's very nice of you.'

'No, it's not. I'm trying to be practical. Apart from the fact that I enjoy your company, of course. In fact, Evie Meredith, you currently comprise my only social life.'

He could raise her mood with one simple sentence. Evie knew in that moment that the longing she was trying her best to bury, would not — could not — be ignored. But she daren't let Jake know that. His personal life still remained shrouded in mystery. He probably regretted having kissed her once, let alone twice!

'Are you still there?'

'Yes, I was just contemplating my wardrobe.'

'Sorry?'

'I left my flat in a bit of a hurry, so, stupidly, didn't pack any clothes suitable to wear for an interview.'

'Really?'

'Believe me! Yes, I'd like to come with you. What time?'

'Pick you up in half an hour?'

'I'll be ready.'

'And don't forget your phone. You need to know when you're wanted in London.'

Evie was changing her blue T-shirt for a white sweater. Her jeans would be fine, tucked into boots and worn with her three-quarter length jade green coat. But first, she needed to apply a little make-up, especially as her mum had mentioned she looked pale. She was ready to step outside the door when Jake pulled up. As she walked down the path, he got out from behind the wheel and came round to open the passenger door.

'Your carriage awaits, m' lady.'

'You are most chivalrous.' She almost

said, 'my prince,' but thought better of it.

They were almost out of the village before he spoke. 'Get much sleep?'

'Not a lot.'

'I slept well, actually.'

'You didn't read my email until this morning?'

'Oh, but I did.'

'Right.' Evie felt a little miffed. She'd been agonising for what felt like most of the night.

'If you don't mind, could we wait to talk until we're in the shop, preferably sitting in the office with a cup of fairly disgusting coffee.'

She chuckled. 'You have a kettle?'

'We do.'

'It sounds as though you're not using the right coffee. I'll see what I can sort out.'

'You're a life-saver.'

They drove on in silence, Evie taking the opportunity to enjoy the scenery. Snow still lay in disconsolate heaps here and there but the roads were pretty clear. She should have no problem driving to London. She took out her phone to check but there was still nothing from her prospective employers.

Jake noticed, of course.

'They're obviously interested in you. Remember, the festive season's a funny time. People ask for last-minute days off. They become distracted.'

As you distract me, Jake Vallance!

Evie longed to reach out a hand and caress the back of his neck where those little black curls rested so temptingly on his collar. Or stroke his cheek. It was still early in the day, but later there would be a dark shadow on his jaw line. He was a very sexy man.

She must not fantasise. She must not spend time brooding over what couldn't be.

★ ★ ★

'I've checked there's fresh milk in the fridge and I'm going to take these two mugs down the street to that coffee shop we passed, while you do what you need to do.'

He reached for his wallet. 'That'll be great.'

She shook her head at the money. 'My treat. Straight black filter coffee or would you prefer something fancier?'

'Nope. The first option, please.' He sounded amused. 'You obviously have strong feelings about takeaway coffee cups. Good for you. I'm trying to be more watchful too.'

At that moment, Evie heard a phone ringing.

'Is that mine?'

'Yep.' His lips twitched. 'But let me take those mugs from you, first.'

Feeling flustered, she dealt with her call while Jake parked the crockery and changed the door sign to *OPEN*. He switched on two lamps which bathed the surrounding area with a golden glow.

Closing the call, she found him in the office.

'Ta-da! I have an interview on Monday. They're seeing five shortlisted applicants.'

'Well done. What time do they want you there?'

'Noon. They thought I was still in London, so when they asked if ten o'clock was suitable, I asked if it could possibly be later. The woman who rang seemed very friendly.'

'Always good to start off feeling like that, and well done you for not being afraid to query your interview time.'

'I need to take control of my life, don't I?'

'Yep.'

Evie watched his Adam's apple quiver as he swallowed. Something was wrong . . . his face looked almost haunted. Was it because of what she'd said? Dare she put her arms around him and give him a hug?

But with the merest shake of his head, he changed the subject. 'What does a man have to do round here to get a cup of coffee?'

She broke the tension with a joke. 'Hey, I'm not your fairy godmother! I'm on my way.' Evie headed through the door just as a man and women were about to enter.

'Oops, sorry.' She dodged out of their way, barely giving them a glance, her thoughts still occupied with Jake's sudden change of mood. What brought that on so unexpectedly?

'We're cool,' said the man. 'Have a nice day.'

'You too,' she replied. The customer had an American accent. Jake would be delighted to achieve a good sale so early in the day.

Mission accomplished, she got through the door of the emporium and put down her cardboard holder on the counter where Jake dealt with payments. She could hear him explaining the origin of a beautiful carved wood table as he and his customers stood beside it, their backs to her.

'As I explained to Melissa on the phone,' he said, 'the local craftsman who created this in the late nineteenth century was well-known for this type of design.'

Evie, how could you have not spotted Melissa?

She walked towards the little group.

'Could I offer you a coffee, sir, madam?'

The American gentleman turned round. 'Are you some kind of psychic, young lady? We hadn't even gotten in the door when we met you coming out.'

Melissa was watching her in a very calculating fashion.

'Jake said he was expecting you,' Evie said. 'Would you like milk — or sugar?'

'No, thanks, sweetie.' Melissa intervened. 'Brad and I both like our coffee hot and black.' She took her drink. 'Any news of Marcus? You know he stayed at my house when he got stranded?'

Was the woman playing games? Anyway, all that seemed a lifetime away to Evie. She really needed to speak to Melissa before talking to Jake about the Marcus incident, but no way did she intend embarrassing him or messing up his sale.

She handed the other mug to Melissa's companion, smiled sweetly and said, 'Enjoy,' before disappearing into the office. She would kill for a coffee and she imagined Jake would too, but they could wait. She'd noticed the beautiful bronze chrysanthemums arranged in a copper vase inside the window needed fresh water, so she headed through the shop again, trying not to make any noise. The flowers were still bright and soon she had them rearranged. Evie carried them back to the display window, not sure what to do next. But Melissa had wandered away from the men who'd reached the money side of the transaction and was heading in her direction.

'I'm intrigued,' the actress said. 'I promise I won't gossip, sweetie, but what made you turn down Marcus's offer of a fabulous fortnight in the sun? He told me that's why he drove down from town. I'd have gone with him like a shot, even if he isn't the man he likes to think he is, but I was waiting for my adorable Bradley to arrive. Of course his flight got delayed so he didn't arrive until yesterday.'

'Marcus dumped me, that's why I turned down his offer. You know that, Miss McDonnell-Brown.'

'Call me Melissa, sweetie. Sorry, I'm terribly bad with names.'

'It's Evie. I didn't take kindly to being expected to kiss and make up just because the next unfortunate lady in his life very wisely left him in the lurch.'

'Well, little Chloe did have an offer she couldn't refuse, according to Marcus. But she was a passing fancy. He's still fond of you, sweetie.'

Evie had heard enough. 'Well, I'm glad I found out his true nature when I did. I need to ask you, Melissa, did Marcus tell you Jake pushed him?'

'He moaned like crazy about it, kept on about being scarred for life! I'm no Florence Nightingale, but even I knew he was making a fuss over nothing.' Her throaty laugh made Brad glance her way, a fond expression on his face.

'However, it was very naughty of lovely Jake to shove him. Were they fighting over you, sweetie? I couldn't get Marcus to tell me what went on.'

'They weren't fighting over anyone. Marcus was saying very unpleasant things about me.' Evie hesitated and took the plunge. 'He also sounded rather ungrateful about your hospitality, which upset Jake so much, he lunged at him.'

'I see.' Melissa was sipping her coffee. 'How very gallant of him. He's obviously crazy about you. You're a lucky girl.'

Evie took a deep breath. 'He felt very aggrieved, but Jake and me — we're not an item.'

'Please don't tell me you're still hung up over Marcus! Not after what you've said.'

'No, of course I'm not. But Jake and I really are just good friends.'

Melissa rolled her eyes.

'Truly we are! Which is why I'm so worried.'

'Worried about what? Do get a move on, sweetie! Brad wants to buy me something else for the house.'

'Marcus is threatening to report Jake to the police for assault. And he's emailed me, saying if I don't accompany him to the Caribbean, he'll carry out his threat. And even though Jake will be able to provide good character witnesses, nobody heard the horrible things my ex was saying about me — and about you, Melissa. It'll be Jake's word against Marcus's.'

Melissa put her mug on the counter, her eyes gleaming. 'Wow, this is pure soap opera stuff, isn't it? Maybe we should write a script together.'

Evie couldn't help but laugh. Otherwise she might have cried.

'Well, it's lucky you've told me that, sweetie. I too have put up with a lot from the less than delightful Marcus. I only took pity on the guy when he rang to say he was stranded, because I was bored, waiting for Brad to arrive.

'Leave it with me. I'll ring him when I get back. I'll need to keep quiet about him badmouthing me, in case Brad hits the roof. But I'm sure he'll understand, when I tell him we girls must stick together and stand up to creatures like Marcus.' She paused. 'Tell your ex you've no intention of going on holiday with him, and if you have any more trouble, you must let me know. Jake has my mobile number.'

Evie thanked her. For some reason, strange as it might be, she felt she could trust Melissa. But how would she explain this conversation to Jake?

15

Jake insisted on getting their coffees, together with two dark and sticky chocolate muffins. He and Evie were sitting in his office, enjoying the delicious experience.

'Except that if I can't get into my ball gown, I shall blame you!'

'No chance. You'll be the perfect Cinderella. It's my trouser length I'm worried about.'

'Which reminds me, when is our next rehearsal?'

He raised his eyebrows. 'So, you've decided on your course of action?'

'Yes, what did you think I would do?' Caught off guard, she'd blurted out the question and now she waited for his response.

He munched his last bite of muffin before answering. 'I haven't known you very long, but I believe I'm right in saying you have no intention of allowing your ex to snap his fingers and expect you to jump through hoops. However, there was always the possibility of your going along with his sleazy little suggestion, just so I would not worry about the boys in blue turning up. It's the kind of thing you, with your sweet nature, would do.'

She stared back at him.

'By the way, you look quite adorable with that little smudge of chocolate on your nose . . .'

His eyes were sparkling. He looked much happier than he had earlier. Could that be because he'd just sold three expensive pieces of furniture to Melissa's American tycoon? Jake was a businessman, but somehow she got the feeling money wasn't a huge motivation for him.

She rubbed her nose with a paper napkin.

'Is that better?'

He smiled. 'Let's fix our next rehearsal time in a bit. Just now, I'd like to talk more about my possible assault conviction.'

Evie folded her arms. 'I need to tell you something.'

'I think I know what it is.'

She didn't like the way he was looking at her. Male pride was something she'd often encountered in her career. She'd need all her powers of tact and diplomacy.

The shop's doorbell sounded. Evie sprang to her feet and held up a hand in warning.

'Don't even think about saying it!'

'How you've been saved by the bell? We still need to talk.' He rose too. She needed to look up at him, but when she saw the tenderness in his eyes, she began to hope her confession might not go down too badly after all.

Jake went into the showroom. Evie sent a text to Kate, explaining that she was in Elmchester, but would be free to visit the manor next day. Next, she sent a message to her mum, asking whether she needed any shopping. She looked through her photographs. Checked for missed calls. Anything at all, rather than contacting Marcus.

Why was that, exactly? She wasn't entirely sure, given that she felt perfectly confident that Melissa would do what she'd offered to do.

And still Jake's reaction remained uncertain.

★   ★   ★

He returned to the office, smiling. 'You must be bringing us luck. I've just sold that figurehead. I'm delivering it tomorrow.'

'The figurehead?' Something was ringing bells in Evie's brain.

'Come and see. She's rather magnificent.' Jake led her across the showroom. 'There's our queen of the waves. What do you think?'

Evie looked at the carved figure, her noble face, her long black hair rippled by the wind, her radiant blue gown flowing around ample curves. 'She's magnificent.'

'She's one of the few to be carved fully clothed. Apparently she was named Lady Miranda.'

'She was in the back of your car that day you noticed me crying.'

'That's right. I'd just bought her in a country house sale. Look, while it's quiet again, why don't you tell me what you and Melissa talked about?'

Evie stuck her hands in her jeans pockets. 'She was actually very helpful.'

'How so?'

She sensed he was on the defensive.

'She asked why you pushed Marcus.'

'And you told her? What did she think of that?'

'She wasn't angry. In fact, she didn't seem surprised. She joked about it being like a soap opera scene and said nice things about you.'

'Did she indeed? But that's not all, is it?'

'To be honest, I'm very worried about what Marcus might do. I don't think you realise how devious he is. I can't bear the thought of him bringing down the law on you. Think of your reputation!'

Jake's expression was grim. 'Leave me to worry about that. What I don't want is for Melissa to take it on herself to tackle him. He'll think I've gone to her whimpering like a frightened schoolboy. Evie, tell me exactly what she said!'

Evie almost told him it was none of his business, but of course that wasn't strictly true.

'It sounds as though those two have history, and I don't mean just the fling I'd heard about.'

'Why am I not surprised?'

'Melissa told me she'd speak to Marcus.' Seeing Jake's expression, Evie held up her hand. 'Let's leave it at that, please.'

He was shaking his head. 'I wish you hadn't interfered. Have you replied to that email yet?'

She twisted her fingers. 'Actually I haven't.'

'Why not?' His voice sounded cold. Distant.

'Because I'm scared, I suppose.'

'The man's a bully, Evie. For goodness' sake, call his bluff and tell him to get lost, or are you waiting for Melissa to act on your behalf?'

'Of course not!' Evie felt heat flood her face. 'Can't you understand I'm worried about the consequences? What if he went to the police?'

'If he does, they'll ask what took him so long. OK, there might be a bruise but it'll be his word against mine.'

'You can do without the hassle. You'd need a lawyer, for a start.' She lowered her voice. 'And we have a pantomime to rehearse. This is my battle, not yours, Jake. I appreciate what you're trying to do for me, but can't you swallow your pride and let Melissa sort things out?'

Evie headed back into the office and sent a short message to Marcus, stating she had no intention of letting him bully her. Then she looked up local transport, found there was a bus back to the village at two pm and told Jake she was going shopping and wouldn't need a lift home.

'We need to fix a rehearsal time,' she said.

He shrugged. 'Might as well get it over with. How about I ring to ask if we can use the meeting room in the pub?'

She felt a pang. He clearly intended to distance himself from her, even though they were still committed to falling in love on the village hall stage. She could shoot Marcus for what he'd done . . . Well, maybe not shoot him, but throwing rotten tomatoes seemed a very tempting option.

'OK, so if I don't hear otherwise, I'll see you in The Wheatsheaf at seven.'

'Evie, this is crazy. You don't need to take the bus. I'll be leaving here soon after Suzie arrives.'

She faced him. 'I've done something that upsets you. It's going to be hard enough rehearsing our lines together, without sitting beside you in your car for half an hour.'

'Thanks' a bunch.' He turned away.

'Just do what you want to do, Evie.'

She was about to remind him not to forget his Prince Charming kit, but decided against it. Instead, she fetched her coat and bag and left him gazing at Lady Miranda.

★ ★ ★

Evie jumped off the bus, after spending the journey staring through the window without noticing the landscape. The only message she'd received was from Kate, confirming their visit to the manor. Evie tried to keep her mind clear but random thoughts kept buzzing at her like bumble bees. She walked down to Lower Mossford, wondering what other method she might have used to frighten away Marcus once and for all.

She also wondered how Jake would respond when, or if, Melissa rang him to report how she'd dealt with Marcus. Evie couldn't control the situation now. And as she walked home, the ache she felt deep inside still indicated something she kept trying, unsuccessfully, to suppress.

It had seemed such a good idea to accompany Jake to Elmchester. And she'd enjoyed the hours spent with him, except for their disagreement.

It wasn't as if her antennae weren't alert to danger. She might have known he'd kick up over Melissa's involvement — and she was proved right, not that it was any consolation.

Now there was a barrier between Prince Charming and Cinderella which mustn't be allowed to interfere with their on-stage chemistry. She felt wretched and it was all Marcus's fault. But why did Jake have to be so stubborn?

★   ★   ★

Jake drove home listening to a compilation of his favourite songs. He was in need of soothing and didn't want to hear the thoughts tumbling around in his head. He'd blown it now with Evie, without question.

Or had he? Maybe there hadn't been anything to destroy. He still wasn't sure what their relationship was and where it might be going.

He wasn't a love-'em-and-leave-'em type. After Lacy was no longer in his life, he'd stayed on autopilot. Maybe he'd be better keeping his emotions firmly under control and not agonising over Evie. Her issues were more recent than his.

But he couldn't get that kiss out of his mind. That kiss in the dark, alone in her parents' house. And the kiss that followed the first one, when he'd wished that moment would go on and on and on.

Now he faced not only tonight's rehearsal, but also the full cast rehearsals beginning on Monday — the day Evie was off to London for her interview. Maybe she wouldn't get back in time. He wasn't sure if he wanted that to happen or not.

The full cast would be rehearsing on and off for the next two weeks. Then they were due time off for good behaviour to spend Christmas with their families before the show on December the twenty-seventh.

He may never see Evie again, after Saturday's final performance. That thought gave him shivers.

★   ★   ★

Evie's mother was in the kitchen when she walked in. 'I got those serviettes you wanted, and the expensive after-dinner mints, also that special liqueur whisky for Da — Whoops!' Evie looked around belatedly for him.

'It's all right, your father's at the driving range.'

Evie raised her eyebrows.

'You know, they hit golf balls one after another. It sounds as if it's like clay pigeon shooting but without the bangs.'

'You two each have so many interests.'

'Would you prefer to find us sitting either side of the fire, watching daytime telly?'

Evie laughed. 'No way. But how you, especially, keep all the plates in the air baffles me.'

'Actually, Evie, I do need to speak to you on that score. Did you eat lunch?'

'Um, I had a chocolate muffin mid-morning.'

'That doesn't sound very sensible. At least I had an apple and a digestive biscuit.'

'Believe me, chocolate is vital when having any dealings whatsoever with the opposite sex.'

'Jake?'

'Don't ask.'

'How about cheese and crackers and maybe a cup of coffee?'

'That sounds perfect.'

'Put the festive bits under the stairs, darling.' Helen was filling the kettle. 'Then we must talk.'

'I'm not sure that's my speciality just now.'

Her mother ignored her, but dropped her bombshell as soon as they began on their snack.

'Evie, there's been a change in the pantomime.'

'You're postponing it until the new year? What a shame! I mightn't be around if I get this job.'

'Not the dates, it's the cast that's the problem.'

'So, who's pulled out now?' She wondered whether Jake had decided to jump ship. Just the thought made her heart behave badly.

'The evil stepmother.'

'Would I know whoever was taking the part?'

'No, but you do know her replacement and I've spent a couple of hours with her today, discussing how we can go forward. Jake's mother is taking on the role. Annie used to act when she was younger and until today, she was our director, so this change presents another problem.'

'This is the domino effect?'

'In a way, yes. We haven't time to faff about, asking people, so Annie came up with an idea.'

'Are you saying she wants you to take over?'

Helen sipped her coffee. 'Mmm . . . very nice. 'I'd have had a go if all else failed, but we've asked Melissa McDonnell-Brown.'

'Oh, heck.'

'What? She's been in so many shows, she must know something about directing, surely?'

Evie nodded. 'Absolutely. It's just that this whole panto thing gets more and more complicated.'

'We don't have time for all that, Evie. We need to pull together. Hopefully, I've got the business side organised so I can fill in, do prompts, help with last-minute costume changes and so on.'

'Oh — trousers.'

'I beg your pardon?'

'Prince Charming's trousers are too short. I offered to try and lengthen them for Jake but we, that is, he . . . '

Her mother reached across and squeezed her hand. 'I could tell something was up. Of course I'll help. I know Annie's no great shakes when it comes to sewing. Get him to drop them in, and I'll take his inside leg measurement.'

16

Jake was already waiting when Evie arrived. 'What would you like to drink? Any excuse!' His smile was lop-sided.

Evie was torn between relief at his relaxed manner and dismay at having to restrain herself from rushing into his arms. But Gareth the landlord was playing a medley of festive songs rather than romantic ballads, which didn't quite fit the mood.

'A lime and soda would be great, please.'

'Coming up.' Gareth selected a glass. 'I switched on the heater in the meeting room earlier. You should be nice and cosy up there for your rehearsal. Just the two of you, is it?'

'I think so. Unless you invited Melissa, Jake?'

He shook his head. 'The thought of a professional actress watching me die a death is not one that fills me with enthusiasm. If you know about Melissa, I imagine you've heard my mother's taking on the wicked stepmother part?'

'Mum brought me up to speed. Sometimes I wonder whether this could be the most ill-fated panto in history.'

'Oh, I don't know.' Gareth placed Evie's drink on the bar. 'Four years ago, Robin Hood managed to rip Maid Marian's gown when they were both hiding from the Sheriff of Nottingham in the forest. You could see her thermal vest. Brought the house down, that did.'

'I can imagine,' Jake said. 'Come on then, Cinderella. Let's show willing.'

He led the way upstairs, where Evie shrugged off her coat and pulled out the nearest chair. 'It's nice and warm in here, thanks to Gareth.'

'Yep.' Jake took off his coat and sat opposite.

'Seriously, Jake, are you going to be OK with Melissa directing?'

'I don't think I have any choice.'

'I can't keep apologising for what I did.'

'Nor do I expect you to, Evie. All I can say is, it'll be good character training. Now, shall we make a start? Begin with that woodland scene again?'

'Yes — but before I forget, did you remember those trousers?'

He slapped his forehead. 'I clean forgot. Wow, so sorry, and after your kind offer as well.'

'Mum says she'll take over. Call round with them and she'll . . . she said she'll, um, need to measure you.'

She could swear he was trying not to laugh.

'How about tomorrow afternoon on my way back from Elmchester?'

'If you don't hear, you can take it Superwoman will be waiting. It's a wonder I don't have a bigger inferiority complex than I already have.'

'Evie, don't torture yourself. You have such a lot going for you. I can't bear the thought of you being unhappy just because one highly unpleasant member of the male species let you down.'

'Thanks, Jake. Quite honestly, I'll be relieved when I can put this whole thing behind me and start afresh. If I don't get the London job, I'll try for the one that would take me to Switzerland for three months.' She reached for her script. 'Ready, steady, go . . . '

★   ★   ★

Next day, Evie felt slightly more comfortable about the pantomime. Her session with Jake had gone well, with each of them remembering their lines. The real test, she knew, would come at the cast rehearsal on Monday night. Scripts in hand would be allowed, though not for much longer. Evie thanked her lucky stars her lines were the least of her worries. She was pleased with both her costumes — but the big fear was how she. would deal with being on stage with Jake.

Body language would be important, as well as onstage chemistry. Had he thought about this? Or did men view things differently? She didn't know, but she suspected she'd soon find out.

She knocked on Kate's door at two o'clock. Her friend was quick to answer and Liam was already in his pushchair. The little boy looked happy and cosy and his mum was full of smiles as she locked up and pushed Liam down the path ahead of Evie.

'How are your rehearsals going?'

'Not too badly, but so far it's only been Jake and me. Next week, we'll be thrown in with a vengeance! I hope I can make Monday, because I'm driving to London that morning for a job interview. It's at noon, so I should be able to get away ahead of the rush hour.'

'And breathe!' Kate's eyes were sparkling. 'I can't keep up! So much has happened since I last saw you. This is the first time we've been able to go out together and here you are, talking about heading off again. If you get this job, will they want you to start before Christmas?'

'If, by some remarkable chance I did get it, I wouldn't start until the New Year.'

'That's something, anyway. So, how are you getting on with the delectable Jake Vallance?'

Evie shot her a quick look. 'We get on.'

'Nothing more?'

'Why should there be? I'm still licking my wounds after my last relationship and I've got far too much on my plate.'

'OK, keep your hair on.'

'Sorry, Kate. Things have been hectic lately.'

'Of course. But Jake could do with some fun and laughter in his life. Wills knows him far better than I do, of course. They've played cricket together and they meet in the pub now and then.'

'I know. I met your husband after that pub quiz when he walked me home. It seems ages ago — I never knew village life could be such a whirlwind.'

'Wills told me how the queen of the soaps turned up, looking glamorous. He also told me he felt sorry for Jake, as she seemed to be making a big fuss of him.'

'Melissa has a bit of a reputation but she's landed a big fish now. He's an American with plenty of money, it would seem. She certainly mentioned the possibility of marriage when she came into St Stephen's while Dad and I were working on the tableau.'

'There are some gorgeous photos in the local paper. None of you, though.'

'I tried to keep out of the way.' But Evie was intrigued. 'When you said Jake could do with some fun and laughter in his life, what exactly did you mean, Kate?'

'Has nobody said anything about Jake's past?'

Evie's head swam. She stopped walking and pressed her mittened fingers to her eyes.

'Are you OK?' Kate stopped too and began jiggling the pushchair as Liam puckered his face.

Evie set off again. 'Sorry, Kate, must've been someone walking over my grave.'

'Hmm. Well, to continue . . . '

'Actually, Kate, I'm not sure you should tell me stuff about Jake. Is this to do with a former girlfriend?'

'I'm afraid so.'

'Please don't think I've gone all uptight on you, but I truly think, if he has emotional baggage, I shouldn't try to find out about it.'

'You care about him, don't you? Whatever you say about nothing going on between you.'

Evie was silent. They'd reached the village street. Before long, they'd pass Jake's house. Kate was right. But she didn't know her well enough to be sure she wouldn't gossip.

'I can't stop you thinking what you want, Kate, but the truth is, I've had some hassle from my ex and I need to get that sorted before I start dating again. Does that make sense?'

'Of course. I'm sorry to hear about your ex and I apologise if I jumped to conclusions.'

'Don't give it another thought. Now, what's our plan? Walk round the grounds, then have tea?'

'It's a nice enough day, so yes, I think so. You might like a wander round the house later, but I'll have to see how this little one gets on.'

Evie was afraid Kate might be wary of what she said now, so started questioning her about previous village pantomimes.

'Of course,' Kate said as they reached the manor's entrance, 'having Melissa directing this year is bound to help ticket sales. She'll be attending all the performances, and you know how people like to get autographs and take selfies when there's a celebrity around.'

'I hadn't thought of that, but you're right.' Evie felt a frisson of panic at the thought of playing to packed houses. Oh dear, she really wasn't cut out for this kind of thing! And with her emotions topsy-turvy, she'd need to work hard not to make a fool of herself.

★ ★ ★

'Thanks, Helen. I really do appreciate your help. You're a busy person and I know Evie's got her hands full just now.'

Helen shrugged her shoulders. 'So many of us have, Jake, including your own mother. Evie will be better when she finds a job, though I wish she didn't have to go through this business of short-term contracts each time.' She carried on unpicking a trouser hem.

'You're her mother. The worrying comes with the job title.' Jake was watching Helen work, fascinated by her nimble fingers.

She glanced up. 'Were you hoping to see her? I'm afraid I don't know how long she'll be.'

'I'm not sure she's that keen to see me, actually.' Jake wondered how he'd managed to blurt that out — and to

Evie's mother of all people.

Helen went on unpicking the thread. 'This isn't the best of times for my daughter. I haven't thanked you for defending her that time.'

'The guy seems to be a ruthless type but I couldn't bear to hear him sneering about Evie. And about Melissa, of course,' he added.

'I hope Evie's seen the last of him but, as for you, Jake, most people in the know are cheering you on.'

'Is it common knowledge, me up-ending Marcus?'

'Oh, I don't think so. But our resident soap star mentioned how gallant you were when she was in the shop the day after it happened. I think word has got around in certain quarters, but I don't imagine the vicar will be calling on you!'

'I couldn't believe it myself! I find that a bit worrying, actually.'

'Your unexpected emotion, do you mean?'

'It's not like me to use violence.'

'Anyone looking at you can see that. But we humans are complex beings. You need to look inside your heart to understand what made you act as you did. Now, I'm really not going to say any more, except to say, think about it.'

He stared at her. 'You understand, don't you? You know my feelings about your daughter.'

Helen smiled. 'I also know how she feels about you. But it seems to me neither of you is ready to go forward at the moment. I shouldn't be talking like this to you. Evie would have me hung, drawn and quartered!'

'I get the impression she wasn't as fond of Marcus as she thought she was.'

'It's easy to become dazzled and infatuated. I'm relieved he acted like he did, actually, but please don't tell her I said so. I didn't like to see her come home looking so downhearted, but now I realise it was mostly hurt pride.'

Jake pictured Evie the day she parked her car in the gateway. After making an early start to go to a sale, he'd had a worthwhile day, was close to home and looking forward to seeing his father's reaction to the magnificent figurehead he'd bid for successfully. When his mobile phone rang, he'd pulled in to answer the call. Another car had parked in the gateway ahead of him and ever since, he'd watched Evie gradually changing back into the girl he knew she must once have been.

But was he back to the man he was before Lacy's tragic accident? People talked about scars, but how long did it take to feel unencumbered and ready to take a chance on love again? Here was someone who might hold a clue or two.

'Do you think I stand a chance — if not now, some time in the future?'

He'd seen that same wistful smile on Evie's face.

'As I said, you need to look into your heart. You'll be thrown together over the next couple of weeks. That will test you both — and I don't just mean your acting skills.'

'This place is brilliant! I'm so glad we got to visit at last.' Evie was pleased she and Kate had got over that first awkwardness.

'Especially the grounds, but you must look inside as well.'

'I will, now I'm here at last.'

'I sent Wills a text and he's meeting us in the coffee shop at three when he takes his break. I hope that's OK?'

'It's great. I must compliment him on the displays, but I really want to be here after dark, when the lights are on.'

'He'll confirm lighting-up time when we see him. If you can stay on, I'm sure you'll enjoy it.'

Evie chuckled. 'Hopefully it'll take my mind off the panto.'

'Everyone will be delighted you've saved the panto from collapse.'

'I'm not sure if I can fool the audience into believing I really am that downtrodden motherless girl who leads such an unhappy existence.'

'But just think of the happy-ever-after. Your handsome prince will claim you and make you his! Who wouldn't want that to happen?'

They turned a corner and saw Kate's husband, Wills . . . in deep conversation with Jake.

17

Evie couldn't help wondering whether Jake was stalking her. But that wasn't fair. This was typical of village life.

'That's interesting . . . ' Kate muttered. 'Did he know you were coming here this afternoon?'

Evie felt exasperated.

'I don't recall mentioning it.'

Kate glanced at her.

'Your cheeks are very rosy.'

'It's cold and I'm not used to these temperatures, remember? I'm a townie.'

'If you say so. Are you going to invite him to join us?'

'He's obviously here to see Wills, but I hope he's remembered to drop off his costume trousers for my mother to alter.'

It was difficult to shut Jake out of her thoughts when she kept coming across him. Wills had noticed them approaching and Kate was waving. Jake glanced their way and she saw his gaze move towards her. Was that a flicker of uncertainty on his face?

'All right, girls?' Wills called. 'We won't be long. Just discussing a bit of business.'

'You're welcome to join us for tea in the cafe, Jake,' Kate said.

Evie groaned inwardly. More polite conversation, with neither able to show their true feelings — they had enough of that during their script readings.

'I just called in to ask the curator's advice and happened to bump into Wills.' Jake hesitated, looking at Kate. 'I called on your mother as planned but she didn't say where you were.'

Evie registered that silence would make her friends more intrigued about the situation between Cinders and her prince in real life.

'Yes, Jake, come and help us eat cake. You know you want to!'

Everyone laughed and Evie felt relieved she'd broken the ice. This awkwardness wasn't pleasant; she felt it was worse, now she knew Jake was keeping something from her. But they hadn't known each other long enough. Maybe he never would confide in her.

'I might even manage to switch Mossford Manor's illuminations on a bit earlier than usual.' Wills winked at Jake.

'My husband will do anything for a slice of chocolate cake,' Kate joked. 'Especially the scrumptious one the cook here makes.'

'Chocolate cake?'

Jake's expression touched Evie's heart. So that's why he'd brought back those muffins. She could imagine him, a schoolboy with that same hopeful look in his eyes.

Was he sent to boarding school? That would explain his confidence, and also the way he normally contained his emotions. She imagined him, biting his lip as he waved his parents off, their car disappearing down a long drive. Going back inside to face hordes of boys, some eager to pick on anyone smaller and more vulnerable. You'd surely need to build an invisible shield in order to survive that situation?

You've got it bad, Evie. For your own sake, you need to keep your own emotions under control.

Wills lifted his small son from the pushchair and Evie watched Liam smile. Wills kissed the tip of the little boy's nose and Liam reached out and rubbed his little mittened hand against his dad's hair. Again, Evie, catching a flash of something that might have been longing on Jake's face, wondered what exactly tortured him. She was convinced now, something significant must have occurred in his past. But, if he'd locked it away, had something brought it to the forefront again?

Still talking, the men followed Evie and Kate. In the cafe they found a table in a quiet corner, Wills handed Liam back to his mum and went off to fetch a high chair.

Evie was seated next to Jake, across from the others. Jake offered to go and hang up their coats and scarves. When he came back and sat down, Evie breathed in his body cologne, that fresh, tingling smell that made her think of pine groves. While the other couple settled their son in the highchair, he reached for a menu and handed it to her, his fingers touching hers.

'Thank you.' Evie glanced down the selection of teas and coffees without actually taking them in. All she could think of was the electricity coursing through her body after that all-too-brief touch.

She sat there, wanting to reach out to him. Wondering if he might be feeling the same.

★   ★   ★

Outside again, Wills hurried off to switch on the festive lights. Already the winter daylight was fading and as Jake, Evie and Kate made their way to the front of the house, more people were arriving, some with school-age children.

The big fir trees either side of the front entrance lit up first. No colours, just a silvery shawl of glittering stars.

'Simple yet sophisticated,' Evie said.

As music, colour and sparkle transformed the surrounding area into the festive fairyland the publicity promised, Evie heard people exclaiming 'Wow.' Children were laughing, running around, checking out their favourite characters. Trees dripped sparkling gems from bare branches and Santa's sleigh, resting on a snowy slope and drawn by eight glittering reindeer, became the magical spectacle of every child's dreams.

'It's fantastic!' Evie clutched Jake's arm. 'So much hard work must've gone into this.'

'It's why I've barely seen Wills lately.' Kate chuckled. 'Liam's definitely underwhelmed, because he's taking a nap. I expect he'll be more appreciative next year.'

'He's been good as gold.' Evie was still slightly breathless after feeling

Jake's gloved hand squeezing her mittened one. The contact lasted a few beats before she hastily removed her hand.

'I think I'd better go now,' Kate said. 'This little one will be crotchety when he wakes up so we'll head back. If you see Wills, can you let him know? I'll text him from home.'

'You must let me drive you,' Jake said.

'Aw, thanks, Jake, but it's not far and we're well wrapped up. You stay and see the lights while you have the chance.'

Evie's emotions ran high. Should she offer to walk home with her friend or should she stay? But what exactly did she expect to happen? Left alone together, did she imagine Jake might take her hand and draw her down that little path dissolving into shadows, with no pretty lights to attract onlookers?

After Kate set off, Jake remained beside Evie, hands clasped behind his back as he gazed at a miniature roundabout dotted with shiny red cars and chubby silver aeroplanes. Evie wondered whether he really wanted to be with her.

If Kate had engineered this situation, Evie wished she hadn't. But as she heard Jake say her name, she turned towards him, anticipating yet dreading hearing him say he needed to leave.

'Evie, there's something I have to tell you.'

She swallowed hard. 'Jake, it's OK, you don't need to stay on. I'll take a few photos, then take a quick look inside the manor.'

'But I want to stay! I have something to say that might explain why things between us are as they are.'

'Could we walk? I don't think I could eat or drink another thing.'

'Nor me,' Jake said. 'Where to?'

'How about we go inside? It's bound to be quiet now the lights are on.'

They climbed the steps leading to the manor's imposing front entrance. Jake held open the door and she walked into the big hall for the first time.

'It's beautiful. I'd kill for some of those paintings.'

'For your flat or for work?'

She loved his smile. Whatever he needed to say, she hoped it would make things easier between them. But how she ached for him to kiss her again. How ridiculous was that?

'For a set. I'd love to work on a series being filmed here.'

He led her down a corridor and into a big drawing room. 'More pictures for you to drool over. We can't sit down but at least it's quiet, and warmer than hanging about outside.'

'I'm listening, Jake.' Evie wandered over to a window. The curtains weren't drawn and several eye-catching displays lit up the winter gloom.

'I'll try not to make a hash of it.' He sucked in his breath. 'In my last year at uni, I met and fell in love with a girl called Lacy. She was American and we both became involved with the drama society.

'I took it to be a whirlwind romance

but as time went by, we both realised it was something more than that and, to cut a long story short, we eventually moved into a flat together. I was lucky enough to find a position with one of the big London auction houses and Lacy worked for a publisher.'

'It sounds good.'

'It was . . . mostly. We spent two years together but there were huge differences between us. Lacy was a party girl. She loved to hit the town, meet friends, dance the night away. While boring old me — I like meals in country pubs, long discussions, and evenings at home. To me, night clubs can't compete with books, music and films.'

Evie knew which lifestyle she preferred. It was probably one reason why her playboy ex moved on to someone new.

Jake was standing beside her now, arms folded, staring at the night sky. Evie couldn't see any stars, only a fingernail of pale moon hanging in the darkness.

'I decided I'd had enough when Lacy wanted us to fly to Canada for a skiing holiday, meeting up with some of her old friends. I don't mind flying and I would have been happy to meet her friends, but winter sports are just not my thing. I'm hopeless, Evie! No way did I fancy floundering around while four-year-olds whizzed past on skis.'

'I understand. I'm happier in the water than on snow or ice. The slope down to our house is enough of a challenge in wintry conditions.'

He chuckled.

'So you didn't accompany her?'

'No, and I quite understood when she arranged for her cousin to join her in Canada. At the time, I truly believed, when Lacy came back we'd try again. I don't flit between girlfriends, Evie. That kind of life isn't for me.'

'What are you trying to say, Jake?'

He turned towards her. One look at his eyes sent her into his arms, like a butterfly to nectar. They stood, hugging each other, and Jake nestled his chin on the top of her head.

'Sadly, Lacy must have acted like her usual daredevil self.'

Evie felt a chill down her backbone.

'She strayed off-piste and before anyone realised, she'd skied straight into the path of an avalanche.'

'She never came back.'

'No. You can imagine how I felt when I got the news that she was missing, suspected — well.'

'I can only try to imagine how dreadful that must have been. I wouldn't dream of comparing the gloom I went through over Marcus with the anguish you must have felt over Lacy.'

He didn't respond, but she felt his arms tighten around her through their layers of winter clothing.

'I won't go into details of what happened afterwards, but I made a decision not even to think about finding someone else.'

'Understandable.'

'Apparently quite a common choice with grieving folks. After a while you begin to recover, even though that makes you feel guilty.'

'You've no need to feel guilt. It sounds as though, even if you'd gone with her and upped your skiing skills, she'd still have pushed the boundaries.'

'Thank you for saying that.'

'I'm glad you wanted to tell me.'

He drew back, still holding Evie in his arms. She looked up and saw tenderness in his eyes.

'I needed to explain what happened, because since meeting you, I've begun to think I'm ready to move on.' He smiled. 'I don't like that expression but I suppose it describes my feelings.'

Evie felt the strangest mixture of joy and apprehension she'd ever experienced.

'Ever since we kissed that time, I've been knocked off course, and now I don't know whether I stand a chance with you or not. I appreciate you've gone through a tough time, Evie. But sometimes I feel as though we're still strangers.'

She nodded.

'So what do we do? Please tell me if I'm in cloud cuckoo land and shouldn't even be thinking about us beginning a relationship.'

18

Jake's ringtone shattered the peace of the beautiful Georgian drawing room.

'I'll switch the darned thing off!' He reached into his coat pocket.

'No . . . no, take the call. I'm not going anywhere.' She moved away, to allow him some privacy.

'Wills — what can I do for you?' Jake made an apologetic face at Evie.

She was standing before a magnificent portrait of an elegant lady dressed in apricot silk and enough diamonds to make onlookers need dark glasses. Back in the early 1900s, the whole outfit probably cost more than the annual wage bill for all the manor's servants put together.

Evie heard Jake say how Kate had intended to ring Wills once she reached home. The one-sided conversation sounded ominous and when Jake called, she hurried to his side.

He held out his phone. 'Wills is worried about Kate. Could you tell him exactly what she said before she left and how long ago that was?'

Evie's heart pounded as scenarios flashed through her mind. But she spoke confidently as she explained Kate's decision to take Liam home and to ring her husband on arrival.

'We'd have told you if we'd bumped into you, of course.' Evie glanced at her watch. 'She must have left at least a half hour ago. Maybe she was in a hurry to get Liam's nappy changed so left her phone in her coat pocket? She definitely said she was going straight home.'

Evie wound a strand of hair around one finger and pulled it across her mouth to chew, something she'd hadn't done since she was twelve. She handed the phone back to Jake who hadn't taken his eyes off her.

'OK, mate.' Jake sounded positive. 'You drive home, check all's well, and Evie and I will walk the way she would have gone, in case she stopped to talk to someone. Does that sound sensible?'

Putting his phone away, he made a wry face.

'We seem fated when it comes to meaningful conversations, but Wills sounds stressed out.'

'Don't be silly, of course we must help him. I wonder if maybe someone invited her in, perhaps for some reason to do with Christmas? I'll try her number, just in case there's some network problem with Wills' mobile.'

But even though Evie let the phone ring and ring, by the time they got outside, Kate still hadn't picked up. Jake grabbed Evie's hand and they hurried down the drive and out onto the pavement, passing a row of cottages whose occupants were unknown to Evie.

'I've no idea where her friends might live. She told me she missed her mates who were at work while she was on maternity leave, but there must be someone who'd know who they are.'

'Wills would, but I don't want to interrupt him. Tell you what, we can call at my place on the way and ask if my mother knows anything. She's bound to have met Kate in the shop.'

'Good thinking. Any tiny detail will help.' Evie was trying to banish negative thoughts. A dark figure jumping from the hedgerow and attacking her friend, then snatching her baby son from his pushchair! It didn't bear thinking about.

Jake jogged down his parents' driveway, unlocked the front door and called to his mother. Annie responded and Jake was soon back.

'Kate has a friend living in the flat above the community shop. Fingers crossed she decided to pop in for a chat. Come on!'

They lost no time and Jake was ringing the bell when a Jeep pulled up. Evie hurried to speak to Wills, whose face was grim in the street lighting.

'What happened?'

For a moment, Wills couldn't find his

voice. Evie reached in and squeezed his nearest hand.

'Everything's tidy. No Kate. No pushchair. No Liam.' He glanced towards Jake, in conversation with a dark-haired girl, a toddler on her hip.

'I was going to ask her mate there if she'd seen Kate. What can have happened to her, Evie?'

'Hopefully she's sitting by someone's fire. I can't tell you how many times I've put my phone down somewhere or switched it off for a meeting and forgotten to switch on again.'

But Jake's conversation was over. 'Kate isn't here, Wills. Anywhere else she may have called?'

Wills drummed his fingers on the steering wheel. 'There's an old lady who lives on the end of our row. Kate pops in on her now and then.' He hesitated. 'I'm not sure what to do next.'

'Go and knock on the lady's door. Evie and I will continue looking as we walk.'

Evie could tell Wills was unconvinced,

but he nodded, turned his vehicle round and drove off.

'Poor man. He's going through agonies. Oh, how I wish I'd walked back with her.'

'It's easy to think the worst. But you mustn't blame yourself. Kate made the decision to walk home on her own and ninety-nine times out of a hundred she'll have been fine.'

But she's obviously not. And if I hadn't been so keen to try and discover what was going on between you and me, I'd have gone back with her.

Will we ever succeed in taking a chance on one another? It's as if we take one step forward and two steps back, Jake thought to himself. He and Evie had watched Wills' rear lights drop out of sight as he headed for Lower Mossford again. He glanced across at the duck pond where strings of fairy lights twinkled on bare branches. An idyllic village scene? Or something from a nightmare?

'What are you looking at?' Evie

stopped wondering if he was going to take hold of her hand and promptly shoved both hers in her pockets.

Jake didn't answer. Evie looked across at the dark stretch of water.

'Please don't tell me you're thinking what I think you are! Surely that's a no-no?'

'Sorry.' He started walking. 'I don't mean to frighten you, but has Kate ever seemed depressed? Has she ever confided worries?'

'Only the normal sort I imagine any young family might have. Wills doesn't earn a fortune and Kate's still on maternity leave.'

'I know they're saving towards a deposit on one of the new houses going up at the other end of the village,' Jake said.

Evie also knew Kate and Wills were torn between trying for a second baby and delaying this while going all-out for the house purchase.

'No way has she ever sounded low,' she said.

'If, and it's a big if, there is no sign of her and still no phone call, Wills must inform the police. She's not the kind of person to take off for a night without warning. Even if she wanted to, she has no car and she has a baby in tow.'

Jake's outside the box thinking had set Evie on the same track.

'But what if she suddenly decided she wanted a night off from routine and rang her mother, asking her to have Liam for the evening?'

'What, borrow her mum's car and set off for Elmchester?'

'Kate could've gone straight to her mother's, driven her mum's car to Kate and Wills' cottage, dropped Liam and his gran off, then driven to town. Maybe someone rang with an invitation.'

'Too contrived. Why not ring Wills? Surely she wouldn't be scared to tell him?'

'You'd think so.' Evie stopped. 'Unless . . . '

Jake stopped too. 'I've heard about

postnatal depression. Is that what you mean?'

'It has to be a possibility.'

They continued walking. Evie reached for Wills' hand and he unhesitatingly clasped hers.

'We need to stay positive. Let's hope there's a simple explanation, but I'm going to keep on looking for as long as it takes.'

They walked on to Evie's house, where she hurried down the path and repeated what Jake had done. But Helen knew nothing either.

Rounding the bend in the road, Kate gasped as she saw emergency lights flashing down at the end of the row of cottages.

'Let's go!' Jake held tight to her hand as they broke into a run.

*   *   *

Evie held out her arms for Liam as his mum passed him to her after he'd been fed.

289

'Hello, little one,' she whispered. He smelled warm and baby-powdered and she thought he was already half-asleep.

'He's had a busy day.' Kate sat down beside Evie. 'I can't apologise enough for all I put you through. You and Jake, let alone poor Wills!'

'Now we know what happened, it seems perfectly logical. If I'd found your poor neighbour in that state, I'd have rung 999 just as you did.'

'And things just went on from there.' Kate stroked her son's cheek. 'I still can't believe how I decided to call on Mrs Clark like I did. It's just that Liam was still asleep and I thought it'd save me popping round tomorrow.'

'It's a good thing you did stop off.' Evie shook her head. 'Who knows what state she'd have been in by the morning?'

'When she didn't answer the doorbell, I knew something must be up. She usually locks up at the back when she has her four o'clock cuppa but she never got there this afternoon.'

'What would you have done if you hadn't been able to get in the back way?'

'Gone home and found the card with her daughter's phone number. She lives in the next village so once the paramedics had everything under control, I nipped home and made the call. But when I got back to Mrs Clark's, she was terribly distressed and wanted me to stay with her so I rang Mum to ask her to look after Liam.'

'So by the time you'd gone off in the ambulance and tried to ring Will to let him know, he was ringing your mum's landline because he couldn't get an answer from her mobile either.'

Kate gave a wry smile. 'Mum was in such a hurry to get here, she grabbed her car keys and coat and got straight in the car. She didn't even tell Dad until later. It was a real muddle!'

'But you must have saved your neighbour's life, Kate. It sounds like she had a nasty fall.'

'So close to Christmas, too, poor lady. But once they do their tests, they'll know whether she can come home or not. Mrs Clark told me she'd be spending the holiday with her daughter so that'll probably happen earlier than arranged.'

Evie glanced at Liam. 'When's Will back?'

'Soon, I hope. He had things to check on, though his assistant's very clued up. But that husband of mine's a perfectionist.'

Evie offered the baby. 'In that case, I'll let you get on. Thank goodness it all ended like it did.'

'Say thank you to Jake again for me, please. I'm sorry if my adventures spoiled your evening.'

'It's not like it was a date! I mean . . . um, we'd almost finished looking round the house so please don't worry about that.'

'What's up, Evie? Did you two have a row?'

'Of course not. Anyway, we had other

things to think about after Wills rang Jake.'

'So it's back to rehearsals. End of?'

Evie caught her breath. 'In many ways, I'll be thankful when the panto's over and done with. But never let it be said we haven't tried our best.'

★ ★ ★

'I'm trying my best, but how the heck I'm supposed to pretend I'm not in love with the girl I fall in love with on stage when we're Prince Charming and Cinderella, given I'm in love with her in real life, I really haven't a clue.'

Jake's sister, having made one of her rare phone calls home, only to find her parents had gone out to lunch, sighed down the phone.

'I understand how you must feel. I think. But even if you're having trouble with your love life, it's fantastic to think you're out there again.'

'Out where?'

She sounded patient. 'Back in the

293

zone. Dating again. You know what I mean, big brother!'

'Evie and I aren't dating. That's the problem. We've been thrown together by this pantomime and we're rehearsing with the rest of the cast now, but on two occasions we've been on our own, I've thought we might reach some sort of understanding, but it's all blown up in my face.'

'I won't ask. But I'm pleased you told me. Do the olds know?'

Despite his anguish, Jake couldn't help but grin at the expression. 'Absolutely not. And don't you dare say anything.'

'I promise. Look, I have to go now, but tell Mum and Dad I rang and I'll catch them again. Christmas Day if not before.'

'Will do. You look after yourself, little sis.'

'I shall, don't worry.' She paused. 'Don't give up on this girl, Jake. Maybe she has demons of her own to fight . . .'

Jake wandered back to the kitchen where he was making beans on toast. His mother had wanted to take a meal from the freezer but he insisted he was happy with something simple.

Obviously Evie had been very upset by her ex-boyfriend but after he turned up and she discovered just how awful Marcus really was, she'd admitted to having a lucky escape. He understood her reluctance to jump out of one relationship straight into another but he sensed something else bugging her.

They'd had two close encounters, each ending as abruptly as Ella's glass coach changed back into a pumpkin. That kiss! Or even those two kisses, both of which were . . . He cleared his throat. Evie hadn't held back and . . . His bones melted at the thought of her soft, full mouth yielding to his.

Jake stirred his pan of beans and took it off the hob. He reached down to the warming oven and rescued his plate of buttered toast shoved inside when the phone rang.

So, if Evie was even a little attracted to him, and was presumably not pining for Marcus, what stopped her from at least giving Jake a chance? The days were counting down until Christmas Day and once the turkey turned into Boxing Day cold cuts, the pantomime actors and their audience would be anticipating curtain up in the village hall.

Was that behind Evie's mood changes? Was she more nervous than she'd admit? She also had her job interview looming. Tomorrow she'd be off to London and, hopefully, would attend rehearsal that evening.

He needed to await his opportunity. But with his track record, was he heading for heartbreak?

19

Evie stood before the ladies' room mirror, touched up her raspberry lip-gloss and smoothed down her skirt. She wore her dark hair tied back and her gold earrings were shaped like tiny old-fashioned movie cameras. They'd been a gift from her parents when she landed her first contract, and she hoped they'd do the trick today.

It was time to return to the reception area. She felt positive. If only she wasn't worried Marcus might have got wind of her application. She'd spoken to a few contacts but no one seemed aware of his schedule. He might already be airborne and heading for his holiday paradise with some unfortunate starry-eyed young woman.

'They're ready for you now, Evie.' The receptionist shook back her glossy magenta hair and smiled at her. 'Would you go in, please?'

Evie rose and picked up her folio. She tapped lightly on the door marked Conference Room and waited for an invitation to enter. Instead, the door opened and she found herself facing Marcus.

He was smiling a smile that didn't reach his eyes. 'Welcome, Evie. Come and take a seat.'

Willing her legs not to turn to jelly and praying her brain didn't turn to marshmallow, she took the vacant chair at a table where an older man and a woman Evie had worked with before, were already sitting. Marcus waited for her to settle herself before taking his place.

'Great CV, Evie.' The older man smiled at her. A proper smile, she noted, still feeling she'd entered the lair of a wild, unpredictable beast.

'So, can you convince us you're the right person to work on this series?'

Evie opened her portfolio. 'This particular era is a personal favourite of mine, so I'd like to show you some stills from sets I've worked on.'

Before she knew it, she was enjoying her interview. The woman remembered her and made it clear she'd enjoyed working with Evie. To her relief, Marcus asked good questions and the older man listened.

Finally, Marcus requested a private word with the candidate. 'Evie and I share some personal history. I wanted her interview to be over first. Now I'd like to check whether she'd be entirely comfortable working with me.'

The other two interviewers exchanged glances and each rose and left the room.

Marcus moved over to the window and stood in silence. Evie sat, hands clasped together, trying to remain calm. He yawned and stretched his arms above his head. 'You interviewed well, darling. But then, I knew you would. With your talent, you could do this job standing on your head.' He frowned and patted his chin as if debating something. 'There's just one problem.'

'Marcus, I'm well aware I . . . '

'Shut up! The problem is, Evie, your refusal to come away with me. As you can see, I've had to delay my trip, and when I discovered you'd applied for this contract, I knew what I must do.'

She stared back at him, frozen with horror.

'So, how about it? Stop this ridiculous charade and fly out with me as soon as I can sort out flights. The job's yours, then, darling.'

Evie stood up. 'I'm sorry to disappoint you, Marcus, but I won't be bought. So you may as well say whatever you wish to your colleagues who have shown me such courtesy today.'

'You try my patience, you really do!' he hissed. 'How stupid can you possibly be?'

'Not as stupid as I was when I became involved with you! Quite honestly, Marcus, I'd rather take a temporary job in the January sales than work alongside you again.' She held up her hand. 'You're a very talented man, but you bully and intimidate people! I'm out of here before I say something I really do regret.'

Evie didn't even reach the door. It burst open to admit the older man and a security guard.

'My office, Marcus. Now, please!'

'What's going on?' Marcus looked bewildered. 'Everything's fine. We were having a little chat.'

'I'm aware of that.' His senior colleague pointed upwards. 'We were listening to your little chat while the camera was recording it. This company will not tolerate that kind of behaviour. Now, do as I say, please.'

Marcus eyed the security guard who was a good six inches taller than he was, and shrugged. Ignoring Evie, he left the room.

Evie's interviewer turned to her.

'I'm so sorry you had to endure that, Evie. I can't apologise enough.'

'It's quite all right. But I'm wondering whether Marcus insisted on my being shortlisted so he could wreck my chances.'

'No way. You were the first to be selected for interview but the last applicant we've seen. I've been hearing rumours about our friend here for some time now and my colleague, Daisy, who I know you've worked with before, tipped me off about you and him.'

Evie nodded. 'Daisy is awesome to work with. So what I've done is drop Marcus in it?'

'Don't worry about that. I'll find a way of dealing with him. You've already mentioned his talent but he has to change his ways. What you've done, Evie, is to get yourself a job offer.'

'Say that again, please.'

He smiled. 'We'd like to offer you a contract for this new series. May I arrange for it to be. drafted and emailed to you as a matter of urgency?'

Still stunned, Evie nodded her head.

He held out his hand. 'I'll take that as a yes.'

Jake arrived at the village hall early. He didn't really expect Evie to contact him but couldn't wait for her to turn up. He didn't fancy acting opposite Melissa McDonnell-Brown. Speak of the devil! Melissa was walking to front of stage. Standing there, saying nothing, while people nudged each other and the buzz of conversation subsided.

'Good evening, everyone. This is a good turnout except for our Cinderella.' She looked straight at him. 'Jake, any news re your leading lady?'

'Only that she was planning to drive back from London this afternoon.'

'Well, if she doesn't turn up in the next two minutes, I'll read in for her.'

Jake sent up a silent prayer. What if Evie had been offered a job where she had to start at once? He'd be devastated, and not only at losing his co-star. Then the hall door opened and Evie entered, still in a smart dark jacket and skirt.

'Sorry, Melissa! I'm sorry, everyone, but I was held up by an enormous set of roadworks.'

Jake relaxed. At least he wouldn't have to be in a clinch with Melissa, as they were doing the full play tonight.

'Shall we begin?' Melissa didn't wait for an answer. 'From the top, so we're in the Baron's kitchen. Cinders, you look far too elegant in that beautiful suit but that's going to test your acting skills, sweetie, isn't it?'

'I'll cope!' Evie set off to join the Ugly Sisters backstage, winking at Jake en route.

She seemed in good form after her busy day. He wanted to find out if she'd got the job but knew he must be patient. Earlier, Jake's parents had revealed something involving their future and his feelings were mixed but he mustn't let personal matters intrude now.

Melissa sat in the front row, clipboard and pen in hand. Jake took a seat further back with others not in the first scene. When Evie entered, he saw she'd taken off her jacket and high-heeled black patent shoes and put on a faded overall and a pair of pumps. Her hair was loose and she looked no more than eighteen, Jake thought, watching her drop her shoulders and bite her lip.

Cinders began on her soliloquy and he relaxed a little more.

The Ugly Sisters burst into the kitchen. This pair, played by two forty-something dads, also members of the village cricket team, made Jake smile as they clowned around. The scriptwriter had trawled for suitable names before arriving at Lavender and Lavinia for no apparent reason. But she had also drawn upon the 2015 update of the original film. It was a clever mix that Jake thought might well amuse an audience used to TV dramas and big movies, simply because it was so well geared to village life and personalities.

As his cue approached, Jake headed through the kitchen where a door led backstage. He arrived just as Evie questioned who might be striding through the trees. Face to face with the girl he loved, he forgot all about acting and spoke the prince's words with total sincerity.

At the end of the scene, several people applauded. Backstage with Evie, he pretended to mop his brow.

'You were great, Prince Charming!'

'Only because of you. Now, how did that interview go?'

'Much better than I thought it would when I first walked in. They've offered me a contract.'

Jake gave her a quick hug. 'Excellent news. Can we talk later?'

'Any particular reason?'

'Yes.'

★ ★ ★

They walked to the village inn after rehearsal, chatting over Melissa's comments.

'She was very positive but how she puts up with us, I don't know.' Jake sounded gloomy.

'She knows we're all amateurs. I'm hoping our audiences will be kind.'

'They will be to you! Everyone wants Cinders to go to the ball.'

'Could we walk a bit slower, Jake? I can hardly keep up!'

He stopped. 'Sorry, Evie. I'm a bit stressed.'

'Well, it didn't show at rehearsal. I thought you did a great job.'

'That's a relief.'

They walked on in silence, Evie unwilling to ask what was stressing him out. He wasn't the only one with something to say, but she'd prefer to have the pantomime done with before revealing what was on her mind.

They walked into the lounge bar. To her surprise, Jake insisted on ordering a bottle of wine.

'We must celebrate your new contract!'

He politely declined offers to sit at someone's table, gaining several whistles and catcalls. Evie knew she mustn't drop her guard. Her split from Marcus was now something to forget but Jake's relationship with Lacy had understandably left him with a lot of grieving to do. How could she possibly hope to take the beautiful American girl's place? The prospect was too daunting.

Jake poured them each a glass of white wine.

'Congratulations on your new job, Evie.' He clinked his glass against hers.

'Thank you. I definitely started on the back foot but I don't want to bang on about it now. What did you want to say?'

'My father has decided to retire.'

Evie gasped. 'I hope his back isn't a major problem?'

'It's much better now. No, he and my mother have decided to do some travelling. He's suggesting I either sell or let my flat in London and settle in Upper Mossford so I can run the emporium — with Susie's help of course. He'll still act as a consultant.'

'So, how do you feel about that?'

'I've asked for time to think. I've enjoyed these last weeks much more than I anticipated.'

'Because you're in the panto?' Evie spoke teasingly but her heart was pounding. Maybe she shouldn't drink any more wine.

'Partly that.' He met her gaze. 'But only because it means spending time with you.'

She couldn't look away. Was this one of those pivotal moments people talked about? The moment when a couple realised they wanted their friendship to become something more? She thought of how she'd felt when he first kissed her. Of course she'd fantasised about how things might develop, but succeeded at last in convincing herself to remain firm.

'You look as though I've confessed to kidnapping Rusty! Is what I've said so very terrible?' He reached across to trap her fingers beneath his. 'You do understand how special you are to me?'

Evie stared down at their linked hands.

'Evie?'

She couldn't say it. How could she possibly confess how frightened she was of causing him any more pain? Far better not to let him say anything else he might later regret . . .

She looked at her watch and gasped.

'Oh my goodness!' She pushed back her chair. 'Jake, I'm so very sorry, but I'd forgotten my brother's due to Skype us tonight. Please forgive me, but I must get back!'

20

How she could survive, acting opposite him for the remainder of the rehearsals, was a mystery. And she must have lost the plot, because she kept checking to see if he'd texted her.

Why would he? She'd drawn the final curtain on romance. Often she lay awake at night, going over that brief time at the pub when he opened up his heart, only to have her snub him. She'd played a nasty trick that was all for his own good.

At rehearsals, Jake said his lines. She said hers. Melissa, whether she knew something was up or not, was an excellent director and all the actors were benefiting. The show would probably be the best one the village had ever put on. And who could possibly suspect that the prince and his bride to be were hiding their secret feelings for each other?

With Christmas looming, Evie became more and more depressed. Even the thought of her new job didn't cheer her up and at the dress rehearsal, Melissa kept giving her strange looks. After the final scene, when the cast congregated on stage around Prince Charming and his princess, Melissa and her helpers gave them all a big round of applause.

When Evie was changed back into her own clothes, Melissa approached her.

'How about coming to my place for a drink?'

Surprised, Evie assumed others were invited too. 'Yes, that's fine, Melissa, but um, is Jake invited? You see, he and I . . .'

'I'm not blind, sweetie. No, Jake isn't invited — in fact no one else, only you. I won't keep you very long, but certain things need saying.'

Evie followed the soap star from the hall, calling goodnight to the folk who turned lights off and locked up.

312

Melissa's house wasn't far away, but she led Evie to a two-seater sports car in the car park.

'Hop in. We'll say hi to Brad, then hunker down in the kitchen with a drink.'

It wasn't many minutes before the two women were in Melissa's enormous, state-of-the-art kitchen.

'Grab a stool, Evie, and I'll open some wine. White all right?'

'Lovely.' Evie watched her hostess whisk a bottle with an expensive label from a wine cooler no one would suspect existed. 'Melissa, have I done something wrong? I don't claim to be an actress.'

Her hostess placed two crystal flutes on the counter and splashed a generous amount into each.

'Cheers,' she said, raising her glass. 'Here's to a successful pantomime. And you, Cinderella, have every right to be taking the leading role.'

'It's kind of you to say so.'

'But you're still miserable as sin.

That's not a question.'

Evie sipped her wine.

'Is it so obvious? I'm trying not to let it interfere with our onstage chemistry.'

'As is your leading man. And it's working, so don't worry about the show. What you should worry about is that Jake Vallance and you are slowly torturing one another. Whose fault is that, I wonder? Come on Evie, take another swig of wine and answer me.'

Melissa was very persuasive and, almost as though mesmerised, Evie obeyed, suddenly realising she'd had enough of pretending she didn't care for Jake.

'It's my fault. I'm the one with the cold feet.'

'But, why, Evie? It can't be because of Marcus!'

Evie shook her head. 'No, it's because I'm frightened of hurting Jake.'

Melissa raised her elegant eyebrows.

'You mean the skiing accident? Oh, don't look so surprised. We live in a village, remember? Even an incomer like me gets to hear local gossip, especially now I've made friends with my cleaning lady and gardener.'

'I don't like to think of people whispering behind his back!'

'Ha! That's more like it. You should have seen your eyes blaze when I was speaking. If I could get that same expression on my face when I'm playing a character whose heart is breaking, I'd be up for an award! You love him to distraction, don't you?'

Melissa topped up Evie's and her own glass. Evie didn't protest.

'I do love him, yes. When I first met him I thought how gorgeous he was. It didn't dawn on me until later that he's also a very kind person. Thoughtful.' She chuckled. 'Very loyal.'

Melissa laughed. 'Yep. Certainly knows how to throw his weight around when required. I imagine he also knows how to kiss a girl?'

Evie felt herself blushing. Melissa held up her hand.

'I can see he does. So, what's holding

you back? It's at least two years since that unfortunate American girl lost her life. A man like Jake needs to move on.'

'I'm afraid I might hurt him in some way. He's probably going to be based here because of the family situation. Please don't tell anyone, Melissa. I don't know if Jake's even made a decision yet.'

'What about?'

'His father's decided to retire and he wants to hand over Vallance's Emporium to him. That'd mean Jake living here, not in London. I'm going back to London in January, to begin a new job. It's hardly the ideal start if we . . . if we were to begin a relationship.'

'You must be joking. Jake's often in London for business reasons. And it's hardly the other side of the moon, is it? You found your way back to Mossford after your interview?'

'Of course. But, I get the feeling Lacy was beautiful and clever and from a well-off family and . . . '

'And she was also selfish. Don't look

so surprised, Evie. I know a little bit about her. Jake got talking to Bradley when Brad called in to collect a purchase he wants to keep secret from me, bless him.'

'Jake seems to feel he was to blame because he didn't go on the trip with Lacy. I told him the accident would probably have happened anyway.'

Melissa shook her head impatiently.

'What-ifs are the pits! Yes, Jake talked to Brad because he needed someone to open his heart to. Sometimes a person's parents aren't the right people to confide in.'

'And what did Jake say?'

'He told Brad he was very much in love with you, but couldn't figure out how he could possibly melt your heart. Jake thinks the time's not right for you to love again — even if it is for him.'

'But that's crazy! Jake's ten times the man Marcus is!'

'Then why don't you tell Jake how you feel? Why miss out on the chance of happiness, knowing he feels the same, but won't put pressure on you?' Melissa wriggled down from her stool and began taking cheese and fruit from the giant fridge. 'We should eat something if we're finishing that bottle of wine. Then Brad will drive you home. You're to get a good night's sleep and start the rest of your life tomorrow. Christmas is a great time for romance. Cinders, you shall go to the ball!'

★ ★ ★

As if her fairy godmother had waved her magic wand, Evie slept well and found birthday cards on the doormat when she went down to breakfast next morning. With every one she opened, she felt disappointed it wasn't from Jake. How silly was that? But after breakfast, while Evie was vacuuming the sitting room, her mother answered the doorbell and called out that a Christmas bouquet had been delivered.

Evie ripped open the envelope, heart thudding in her chest. She recognised the handwriting from the notes he'd written on his script. His message was brief

Wishing you a very Happy Birthday and a Joyous Christmas, Cinderella.

She didn't deserve such a gorgeous bouquet. Red roses must cost a fortune at this time of year. And there were snow-white chrysanthemums and frothy greenery, all tied up with shiny silver ribbon.

She ached to see Jake. Her mother made no comment but there was no mistaking her smug grin as Evie rushed to find a suitable vase.

For the first time since that horrible night at the pub, Evie sent Jake a text.

Thank you. I have so much I want to say. She hesitated and added a kiss.

He replied at once. *Likewise, but the time's not right yet. The show must go on.* He'd added a kiss too.

Evie pressed her phone to her cheek. They understood one another. And the best was yet to come. She was sure of that now.

Jake had plenty on his mind. Most importantly, he'd had a tough time with an unexpected new friend. Melissa's American beau was far older and wiser than Jake, and he was obviously fast learning about English village life. Over a couple of pints of local ale, Bradley had told Jake not to be a fool and confided he, too, knew he'd met the woman of his dreams and intended proposing to her.

'But I can't do that!' Jake had protested. 'We haven't known each other very long. Besides, she's hardened her heart towards me.'

Brad had used quite a rude Americanism.

'I know for a fact that young lady's head over heels in love with you.'

'You can't possibly know that.'

His new friend had smiled. 'Wanna bet?'

Suspecting Melissa's hand in this, Jake had ordered flowers for Evie. And waited.

Her text message filled him with joy. Deep down, he'd always felt the attraction between them was powerful. But his parents were entertaining family members and, with Jake's sister abroad, he must delay his real-life wooing.

So Jake ran the family business single-handed on Christmas Eve, returned home after closing at four o'clock and carried out his elder son duties. He escorted his mother and his aunt to Midnight Mass and found himself strangely affected by the silvery sound of the bells as he walked towards the church. Once inside, he spotted Evie sitting in a pew beside a tall young man. His heart had almost leapt into his throat. But the young man with the coppery curls had turned his head and Jake realised he was almost a carbon copy of his twin sister.

Evie's wistful smile in his direction gave Jake's heart a further excuse to misbehave. He'd walked towards their pew to greet the family, allowing Evie to introduce her brother, Ed, who'd flown home from America the day before.

'We'd better get our lines right on Boxing Day!' Jake's comment caused the Merediths to chuckle and he'd excused himself and gone to join his own family. Candles were lit around the church and he marvelled at the beauty of the Nativity scene, so carefully constructed by Evie and her father.

Somehow he got through Christmas Day, which brought extra guests for the special festive meal. He sent a text to Evie, saying, *Will you be at the palace tomorrow?*

Her response read, *I don't have a ball gown!*

Boxing Day couldn't come fast enough for Jake.

★   ★   ★

The Mossford pantomime cast played to packed houses. That first woodland meeting between Prince Charming and

Cinderella set the tone for the rest of the performances.

But only after the final curtain call on Saturday night did Melissa congratulate her actors. When Evie was changing out of her turquoise blue ball gown, the soap star had arrived backstage to tell Evie how well the sparks had flown between Cinders and Prince Wotsit.

'Drinks and nibbles all round,' Melissa called to everyone. 'Bradley's in charge of the bar, people, so get a move on!'

Evie slipped on a little black dress and wrapped a sea-green scarf around her shoulders.

Jake appeared at her side as she stood in the queue for the fruit punch served by Brad, as everyone now called Melissa's American.

'You were amazing,' he whispered.

Evie shivered as his warm breath tickled her ear. She felt they were on the verge of something wonderful. Something she'd never dreamed would happen. Magic had been created on stage over the last few days. Could that same magic transform her and her real life Prince Charming?

Jake kissed her on the cheek. Evie didn't care if anyone was watching. This felt right. A huge sense of relief was flooding her body.

'I wanted to suggest we went back to my place. I've taken over what used to be the granny flat.' He watched her smile. 'Don't you dare laugh! It makes a perfect bachelor pad and it means I have privacy.' He paused. 'But I wondered whether you might suspect my intentions, Evie.'

'What? With our track record!' She sipped her glass of punch. Things were happening fast between them and she was happy to go with the flow.

'Yeah.' He grinned. 'We seem to have a habit of plunging the house into darkness or causing phones to ring. Mind you, the former mightn't be a bad option!'

'Naughty boy,' she scolded.

He put his arm around her waist. 'So

shall we slip away and continue this discussion in private? It's time we stopped pretending and started talking about what we both want, don't you think?'

* * *

Walking through the cold night air, Evie thought how beautiful the sky looked and how she would never tire of its starry canopy. Jake held her hand tightly and within minutes they were crunching over the gravelled drive towards his house. An exterior light came on, but he ignored the front entrance and let them in through a side door.

Inside, he switched on lamps and Evie was looking at a pleasant room, furnished in the style she'd have expected Jake to favour. Uncluttered. Muted colours. There was a huge cream sofa with a scattering of green and blue cushions.

Evie unbuttoned her coat while Jake

delved into the sideboard and produced a bottle of red wine and two glasses.

'Are you warm enough?'

'Oh yes. It feels cosy in here.'

'Make yourself at home. Shall I pour the wine?'

'In a bit. Jake, can we just talk?'

I don't need entertaining. I need to know how you really feel.

'Of course.' He took her hand and walked her over to the sofa.

She deliberately sat close to him.

'This is nice.' He placed his arm around her shoulders.

'It is.' She snuggled even closer.

'Let's make it even nicer.' Gently he tipped her chin upwards and Evie relaxed in his arms as their lips met in the most delightful way.

She knew he desired much more, as she did. But they were here to talk. Not to rush things and risk spoiling the moment.

'Why don't you tell me exactly what your new job entails?'

'I'll be based in London, so I'll be

living back at the flat, certainly at first.'

I shan't be going for the Switzerland contract, now I'm committed to the London job. Suddenly she knew she really didn't want to travel too far away from Jake.

'How can I say this?'

'Just tell me what you want, Jake.'

'I want you, Evie. If you'll have me.'

They didn't talk for a while.

'So, will you come back here some weekends? And let me come and see you in London?'

'You've accepted your father's offer?'

He kissed the top of her head. 'I've known for a while that I'd be the one he'd hand his beloved enterprise over to. My sister wants to work abroad for a few years.'

'You travel when necessary, don't you?'

'Of course. But with you in my life, I'd stay in London or come back here, depending on where you were.'

That deliciously warm feeling was spreading further and further. 'May I ask you a question?'

'Ask away!'

'Why are we still talking?' Evie turned her face towards him.

He pulled her even closer and she looped her legs across him so he could lift her on to his lap. Evie closed her eyes and relaxed into his kiss. If there were bells ringing, this time they signalled her joy at knowing she and Jake were following the same script — even though there'd be a lot of juggling for them to make a go of their relationship.

'I love you, Jake.' The words were out before her brain could catch up with her heart.

'And I love you, Evie.'

'I can't believe how hungry I feel now!' Her good intentions were dangerously close to crashing and burning.

'Me too.' His voice sounded husky. He smoothed a wayward copper curl behind her ear. 'How about I make us my speciality? Beans on toast and a pot of tea.'

'Perfect. And I'll tell you how we can finally put the Marcus problem behind us. It's important you know what happened at my interview, but in future I shan't ever mention his name again.'

She scrambled off his lap. He got up and took both her hands in his.

'Before we grab some supper, I want you to know I don't think Lacy and I would have lasted, given our two personalities. I want you, Evie.'

What she whispered in his ear made him groan and pull her close.

'Don't ever feel you shouldn't mention Lacy to me. She was once an important part of your life.'

He was kissing her again.

'Goodness, it's midnight already,' she said when they finally reached the kitchen.

'And this time, we'll keep the magic alive, Cinderella!'

We do hope that you have enjoyed reading this large print book.

Did you know that all of our titles are available for purchase?

We publish a wide range of high quality large print books including:
Romances, Mysteries, Classics
General Fiction
Non Fiction and Westerns

Special interest titles available in large print are:
The Little Oxford Dictionary
Music Book, Song Book
Hymn Book, Service Book

Also available from us courtesy of Oxford University Press:
Young Readers' Dictionary
(large print edition)
Young Readers' Thesaurus
(large print edition)

For further information or a free brochure, please contact us at:
Ulverscroft Large Print Books Ltd.,
The Green, Bradgate Road, Anstey,
Leicester, LE7 7FU, England.
Tel: (00 44) **0116 236 4325**
Fax: (00 44) **0116 234 0205**